"Alexi…" She Whispered
In Her Sleep, "I Need You.…"

Bracing himself against the dangerous need rocketing through his body, Alexi bent and eased Jessica, complete with pillow and blanket, into his arms.

She snuggled against his chest and Alexi didn't move, forcing his breath to slow. With her defenses down, Jessica looked young and sweet and innocent.

An involvement with this woman would only bring frustration and pain.

Wanting to rid himself of the danger of this woman, Alexi carried her back to his bed, lowered her slightly and let her fall the last inch. He did not want to touch her in his bed.

He could not touch her.

Alexi clenched his fists and closed his eyes. He sat in the chair and brooded the curse of Chief Kamakani over Amoteh.

Because it was surely the chieftain's curse that had brought Jessica Sterling anywhere near Alexi.

Dear Reader,

Welcome to another passion-filled month at Silhouette Desire—where we guarantee powerful and provocative love stories you are sure to enjoy. We continue our fabulous DYNASTIES: THE DANFORTHS series with Kristi Gold's *Challenged by the Sheikh*—her intensely ardent hero will put your senses on overload. More hot heroes are on the horizon when *USA TODAY* bestselling author Ann Major returns to Silhouette Desire with the dramatic story of *The Bride Tamer*.

Ever wonder what it would be like to be a man's mistress—even just for pretend? Well, the heroine of Katherine Garbera's *Mistress Minded* finds herself just in that predicament when she agrees to help out her sexy-as-sin boss in the next KING OF HEARTS title. Jennifer Greene brings us the second story in THE SCENT OF LAVENDER, her compelling series about the Campbell sisters, with *Wild In the Moonlight*—and this is one hero to go wild for! If it's a heartbreaker you're looking for, look no farther than *Hold Me Tight* by Cait London as she continues her HEARTBREAKERS miniseries with this tale of one sexy male specimen on the loose. And looking for a little *Hot Contact* himself is the hero of Susan Crosby's latest book in her BEHIND CLOSED DOORS series; this sinfully seductive police investigator always gets his woman! Thank goodness.

And thank *you* for coming back to Silhouette Desire every month. Be sure to join us next month for *New York Times* bestselling author Lisa Jackson's *Best-Kept Lies,* the highly anticipated conclusion to her wildly popular series THE McCAFFERTYS.

Keep on reading!

Melissa Jeglinski

Melissa Jeglinski
Senior Editor, Silhouette Desire

Please address questions and book requests to:
Silhouette Reader Service
U.S.: 3010 Walden Ave., P.O. Box 1325, Buffalo, NY 14269
Canadian: P.O. Box 609, Fort Erie, Ont. L2A 5X3

Hold Me TIGHT

CAIT LONDON

Published by Silhouette Books
America's Publisher of Contemporary Romance

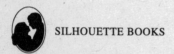 **SILHOUETTE BOOKS**

ISBN 0-373-76589-4

HOLD ME TIGHT

Visit Silhouette Books at www.eHarlequin.com

Printed in U.S.A.

Books by Cait London

CAIT LONDON

is an avid reader and an artist who plays with computers and maintains her Web site, http://caitlondon.com. Her books reflect her many interests, including herbs, driving cross-country and photography. A national bestselling and award-winning author of category romance and romantic suspense, Cait has also written historical romances under another pseudonym. Three is her lucky number; she has three daughters, and her life events have been in threes. Cait says, "One of the best perks about this hard work is the thrilling reader response."

One

Alexi Stepanov decided to let his stalker catch him. At thirty-three years old, he was tuned to his senses and used to hunting in Wyoming mountains. A slight chill penetrated the tinted glass window to touch his skin—or was that chill running up his nape because someone was watching him?

He stood inside the sprawling Amoteh Resort. The luxury hotel's massive windows faced the night and southern Washington's Pacific Ocean.

At one o'clock, the resort lay hushed, the social area's massive pool reflecting the water waves upon the ceiling. In January, only a few guests were vacationing at the resort. Kitchen facilities had been cut to an informal buffet style, a far cry from the elegant dinners served during the busy season.

Outside, the night brewed a winter storm, predicted to bring a mix of rain, sleet and possibly snow. Like a beast, hungry for land, the storm was moving in over the huge, black wind-tossed waves toward shore. Intermittent lightning skimmed over the tops of the churning clouds and the only sound in the huge room was the sound of water lapping at the sides of the pool.

After a day of remodeling the old house where Alexi's father would retire, the Amoteh suite provided the welcome comforts of a luxury bathroom and television. Courtesy of Mikhail Stepanov, manager of the resort and Alexi's cousin, Alexi was temporarily using the manager's private suite; Mikhail was at home with his wife and daughter.

Could he find peace in this small oceanside community?

Alexi inhaled sharply. On previous visits to his aunt and uncle, and his cousins, Mikhail and Jarek, Alexi had found that he enjoyed the town, also called Amoteh. In Wyoming, there were too many reminders of how his dreams—and his pride—had been strangled—by a woman who wanted more, always more.

As Alexi waited for whomever had been following him to come nearer, a ripple of danger seemed to move through the huge potted tropical plants at his side. He nudged aside a child's forgotten ball with his boot. If he were attacked, the ball could cause him to lose his balance.

The person who had been stealthily following him could be dangerous. His shearling coat was more suited to the mountains than to this more moderate climate and it could encumber him in a tussle. The thick padding could also protect him from a man Alexi and his brother, Danya, had forcibly removed from this small oceanfront town—a very dangerous man with a grudge against the Stepanovs....

A flash of lightning lit the grotesque masks on the totem poles outside the resort—a reflection of the Northwest Pacific's Native American heritage—and Alexi thought about the past week.

Someone was riffling through the details of his life; a woman's voice had queried several people in Venus, Wyoming, about her old boyfriend, Alexi. The name the woman had used when speaking to his father and his brother didn't really matter; it was probably false. She had supposedly reached the wrong number—striking up a conversation with the new owners of Alexi's ranch. The innocent pretext led to a seemingly friendly conversation that released too much of Alexi's personal information.

She had asked if he was seeing anyone. *Was he seeing anyone? Not likely, not after a woman had taken everything she could from a man, including his pride.*

Alexi frowned slightly as a light, cold rain began to hit the ceiling-to-floor windows in the resort's pool and social area room. Like tiny snakes flowing to join others, the rain slid down the glass as he thought about his ex-fiancée, now another man's wife. A model bent on a runway career, Heather Pell had moved on to bigger opportunities provided by her millionaire husband.

Three years ago Heather had returned Alexi's ring and his dreams in a cold note that said she didn't "want to be stuck on a godforsaken ranch for the rest of my life."

He'd put almost everything he'd saved into building the home she wanted, into the ranch he wanted. *Did he love her?* Alexi didn't know now. Looking back, he hadn't been thinking about love that much at the time. Maybe he was so entranced with his pictured dreams of marriage, home and children that he hadn't seen the reality of what their relationship was missing—a love like his parents.

In the end he'd sold the ranch at a loss and was glad to be rid of the house his ex-fiancée had designed. Unable to settle into new goals and dreams, Alexi had taken the opportunity to remodel a home for his father and to visit his cousins in Amoteh.

Burned by his ex-fiancée, Alexi had decided to leave attachments of the heart to other men; he wasn't stepping into that cow pile again, asking for more pain.

Restless with his thoughts and more comfortable in nature's elements, Alexi opened the resort's door and stepped out into the night. He decided to lead his stalker away from the Amoteh Resort; he wanted no trouble within his cousin's luxurious domain.

As Alexi moved through the dormant but manicured gardens, he took the wooden steps downward. They led toward Amoteh the town, which was fed by tourists in warmer weather. Walking slowly, making certain that he could be followed easily, Alexi moved away from the resort. The resort's exterior lighting framed the huge painted totem poles and Alexi glanced at the eerie shadows thrown against their masks—and the person moving through them, following him.

His stalker was small and quick, agile, too.

Alexi's senses tightened as rain, changing to a mix of sleet and snow, lashed his face. He left the resort's steps and moved onto a footpath, which led to his father's retirement home.

Home? Not yet. In the process of gutting the old house, Alexi wanted it livable by late spring. His father could relocate, enjoy the summer fishing and spend the winter sharing the Stepanov immigrant brothers' stories with Fadey—next to a blazing fire.

The storm hit Amoteh's brown sandy beach in a furious crash of waves. Snow fell steadily now, topping the piles of driftwood and tall beach grass. The path led half a mile northward over sand and brush and ended with wooden steps that had to be replaced, a sprawling back porch that was rotting and cluttered with old discarded cabinets, doors and windows. But the house overlooking the Pacific Ocean was sound and, despite cosmetic problems, the skeleton was based on sturdy cedar beams.

Alexi glanced at the ocean, the winds catching the waves, sending sprays from the whitecaps. Violent, elemental, the water called to him, perhaps to his dark, brooding side that few people had ever seen.

If he decided to buy the Seagull's Perch, a local tavern, he might settle permanently in Amoteh….

Alexi opened the weathered door and stepped inside the house's sunroom. The plastic he had installed over the open windows rattled, protesting the rising wind.

He waited in the cold darkness; the creak of the wooden porch told him the stalker didn't match his weight. His visitor might be trained for other work—

When the door creaked and opened, Alexi held his breath. The stalker stepped inside the open door and Alexi kicked it shut. "Looking for something?"

"Alexi?"

He'd recognize that soft, husky female voice anywhere…and that scent amid a storm of other ones. At the resort's New Year's Eve dance one week ago, held for locals and for guests, he'd danced with Jessica Sterling, a guest at the Amoteh.

At around thirty, Mrs. Jessica Sterling—widow of the Sterling Stops magnate—had a feline grace, gliding and sensuous. She had walked slowly through a crowd of people to find him at the seafood buffet. Her face had been in shadow, her silhouette framed by the light behind her. Her hair had been pinned into a neat chignon and that long, slender neck led to gleaming bare shoulders. The black dress had been long and formfitting, clinging to her hips. Her long emerald-chandelier earrings had caught the light, glittering and swaying along her throat as she'd moved toward him.

As she had moved closer, the thigh-high slit in her dress had revealed a gleaming smooth leg before it fell to those wellkept, polished toes in her strappy high-heeled sandals. As Alexi's gaze had moved upward, he'd found a neat waist and only two tiny straps holding up the low-cut bodice and the smooth-flowing softness within.

In contrast to her sophisticated look, Mrs. Jessica Sterling had carried the scent of soap and fresh air, not Parisian perfume. But her unique scent had disturbed Alexi on a level he didn't want—her scent was that of a woman, exotic and feminine.

Just two feet from him, she'd stopped and slowly looked him up and down. Inches shorter than his six-foot-three height, her high heels lessened the distance between those slanted, mysterious green eyes and his own. "Alexi Stepanov? I'm Jessica Sterling. Would you like to dance?"

The next day she'd come to the Seagull's Perch, where he'd been filling in for the vacationing bartender. The owner would soon be retiring and Alexi was working to get the feel of the tavern—balancing his past life against a new one—and the money it would take to make a start in Amoteh. Jessica Sterling wasn't the barroom type; her long, all-weather raincoat had covered an expensive woolen sweater and slacks. In her brief visit she'd ordered an expensive white wine from Rita, the waitress—but Alexi knew Jessica was studying him as he worked behind the massive walnut bar.

He'd thought at the time that a woman like her—one who would walk through the night alone to a tavern filled mostly with men—would do nothing but cause trouble.

Now, in the cluttered sunroom amid the scents of freshly cut wood, he caught the fragrance of a woman—

"Alexi Stepanov?" Jessica asked in that same husky voice she'd used to invite him to dance—like the rasp of silk falling, gliding along that curved body to pool at the floor. Tonight her hair was covered by the light designer jacket's hood, her legs by slacks that probably cost far more than a good bull calf.

Alexi picked up a flashlight and she winced when the beam hit her face. Her emerald stud earrings caught the light and flashed back at him. "Well, Mrs. Sterling? Did you lose something?"

"Turn that flashlight off." The command came quick and hard, issued by a woman who ran a corporation and who was used to having her orders followed.

Alexi deliberately took his time as she shielded her eyes with her slender pale hand, and an enormous set of emerald wedding rings shot off sparks. Below that hand lay creamy skin and lush full lips, perfectly outlined and gleaming with gloss, but tightened now with anger.

She'd had green eyes, shadowed and mysterious. They had a slow, seductive way of looking at a man—appraising him— that told him that she knew her appeal and how to use it....

Alexi hooked a finger into her hood and tugged it back. A heavy fall of waving hair framed her face and shoulders. A reddish curl caught momentarily on his finger—vibrant, fragrant, seductive, fragrant, soft—like the woman.

Jessica Sterling was exactly the kind of woman his ex-fiancée had been—a pretty, expensive package with a self-satisfying cash register for a heart....

Jessica had danced silently in his arms, looking away from him, her expression unreadable.

But yet, Alexi had sensed that she was circling him, her body yielding to his direction, her waist small and unbound.

There had been no mistaking that genuine softness against his chest and his instincts had told him to press her closer...to take in the rich feel of this woman with a slow sweep of his open hand slightly downward to feel the movement of her hips flowing beneath his touch....

The touch of her had haunted him—

Alexi clicked off the flashlight. He had only glimpsed her face before he moved to click on the battery-driven lantern, but the unsettling impact remained. Beneath the flattering tints and the mascara, her green eyes had flashed up at him, filled with the hot burn of temper.

She didn't know Alexi. Why would she already dislike him?

Jessica stayed in the shadows of the gutted sunroom, taking in the table saw, the generator, rough workbench and the massive toolbox. Alexi sensed that she was studying him carefully, circling him—

A rich widow out for fun with a Wyoming cowboy wasn't on his agenda. "Let's have it," he said briskly. "Why did you follow me here?"

In the dim light of the unfinished sunroom, her shadow moved on the rough walls stripped of damaged drywall panels. Outside, the mix of weather had changed again, as restless as the woman. Lightning outside the plastic-covered windows lit her face. Her lids were lowered, the length of her dark lashes creating fringe shadows down her cheeks. She ran her manicured hand along a smooth pine board and lifted her face to him. "You're going to be difficult, aren't you?"

"Depends. You've been researching me for this past week. Why?"

Those green eyes caught fire and then slid downward, shielding her expression. Alexi reached out to capture her chin and lift it. "I asked you a question."

Beneath his thumb, her skin was creamy and cool with mist. The scent of rain clung to her, fresh and even more alluring than perfume. But he felt the heat beneath the surface, the nick of anger as she tensed, her eyes slowly opening to his, boldly holding his. He didn't intend to stroke that flawless cheek, surprised as his thumb moved, contrasting the texture and color of this woman's fine skin.

"I'm not ready to answer," Jessica said slowly, huskily, as she raised her hand to push his away from her face. She stepped back as though she disliked being too close and, taking her time, circled the room. Rooms without doors led off the main room. A damp, chilly draft lifted a curl beside her cheek and she impatiently brushed it away.

She walked around the buckets that caught rain dripping from the ceiling. "Nice. You're remodeling this for your father. He'll probably want some kind of little shed, some livestock in the few acres attached to this place…maybe a garden. A man from the country usually wants those things. Why are you remodeling this place, and not your brother? Didn't Danya want to come? Or did you need to get away from Venus and a love gone wrong? Your fiancée married someone else, didn't she? That must have been difficult for you. Is that really the reason you're in Amoteh, remodeling this place and tending bar? Changing your life?"

Alexi resented her prowling through his life, his emotions, and pinpointing his plans. "You tell me. You're the one who's been researching. You called some friends, pretending we'd been involved. If I checked the resort's records, your outgoing calls would probably coincide with the calls to Wyoming. You should have tried my cousins, Jarek or Mikhail—they live right here. But then, you didn't want them to know that you were asking questions, did you? It was safer to use another name…what was it? Mimi Julian, wasn't it?"

Jessica shrugged away his question and turned to him. "I wanted to see if you were the right man for what I have in mind. I know that you'll be staying here, working on this until you have it livable. From the looks of it, you'll be a while."

She shivered slightly, but stepped over a mound of odd wood pieces and walked toward a doorway leading into the kitchen and pantry area. She lifted aside the temporary plastic and looked inside the darkness. Though still without plumbing and cabinets, the room overlooked the ocean. There Viktor, Alexi's widowed father, could sip his Russian tea and watch the waves, feeling as if he had a little bit of his homeland.

Alexi watched her move back toward him, graceful, purposeful, taking her time before she hit her target. What did she want?

He shrugged mentally, and thought of other times that women on the prowl who were fascinated with the Western male image had approached him. What did she want, other than the obvious—a rich widow wanting a little playtime, a little physical diversion before she went back to the suit-clad corporate world?

The wind pushed at the plastic he'd tacked over the sunroom's old windows, howling around the corners of the house as Jessica came to stand in front of him.

She tilted her head and a long waving length of chestnut hair slid to her throat.

Alexi resisted the urge to ease that gleaming strand away from the pale smooth length, and met her searching look.

Those dark green eyes studied him coolly as she tapped her finger on a length of board. "You think I want you for a lover, don't you?" she asked quietly. "Well, I don't. I'm not in the market. This is business."

Women like Jessica Sterling were usually motivated by business. It ruled their lives. Alexi nodded and said, "I'm listening."

"You're wondering why I'm here. I'll answer—I need someone exactly like you, and you're on site, so to speak. You know the people in Amoteh and they like you. Last year you and your brother, Danya, came into town to visit Mikhail and, gee whiz, when you left, so did a real mean troublemaker, Lars Anders. I think there is a connection between your departure and his. His removal from Amoteh was quiet and neat and Lars hasn't been back since. Then there was the little girl who was kidnapped and saved by you, the publicity kept at a minimum to safeguard her privacy. There were one or two incidents in your local newspaper's archives, including your support of an abused women's shelter—and I'd say that was more than financial support. It probably included a little muscle."

She stuck her hands in her pockets and shivered. "It's freezing in here.... I think you'd be perfect for what I need done. You can be discreet, quiet—and if you take the job, well-paid. Are you interested?"

Alexi Stepanov would be perfect to safeguard Willow, Jessica's friend.

Like the other Stepanov males Jessica had met, Alexi was absolutely trustworthy, an ethical man, one with old-fashioned values.

But Alexi had bitter edges encircling him and she sensed his immediate distrust. Why?

Towering over her five-foot-eight inches, Alexi's lean muscular body was sheathed in a shearling coat, worn jeans and well-worn laced workman's boots. In a hard-weathered face, those narrowed cold, gray eyes, locked jaw and firmly pressed lips said he didn't like her.

He didn't have to; he just had to do the job she needed—to protect Willow.

The wind howled and Jessica tried to forget her chilled body; she hadn't expected he'd lead her so far—"You intended me to follow you, didn't you?"

He nodded, his dark brown waving hair gleaming in the lamplight. The shaggy length just touched his shoulders, a contrast to his neatly clipped cousin, Mikhail. The waves did nothing to soften his jutting facial bones, those fiercely drawn dark brows.

Alexi's hard expression now revealed none of his other cousin, Jarek's, easygoing qualities. According to Amoteh gossip, Mikhail and Jarek doted on their wives and children and loved their parents, Mary Jo and Fadey Stepanov. From what Jessica had seen of Alexi playing with the children and laughing with his relatives, he was also a family man.

In contrast, his defenses had definitely been raised when they had danced, a silent cold shield seeming to drop between them.

His eyes had caught her. In the brighter light between the New Year's Eve dances, they were a cold, brilliant blue. But in the shadows, the shade had become silvery, almost like ice—or steel.

At the tavern he'd moved expertly behind the massive bar, the variety of bottles glittering on the shelf behind him, the mirror reflecting that hard face—the stare directly into her shaded corner, penetrating the privacy she wished while observing him....

She'd almost felt the waves of his dislike across the music of the jukebox, the ocean churning outside, the men talking quietly.

But that didn't concern Jessica, only the need to protect her friend Willow. "If you knew enough to lead me here, you knew I wanted to talk with you. We could have had this conversation at the resort, but instead, you had me follow you. You prefer your terms, you like to be in control, and you're perverse, Mr. Stepanov."

"No, just careful."

"You're more than that. You don't trust me, do you?"

His nod was curt, those blue-gray eyes cutting at her in the dim light, appraising her. His disdaining gaze ran down, then up her body. She knew what he saw—expensive clothes, a woman used to spas and wealth and getting what she wanted.

And she wanted him.

"You could say that," he said in that deep careful drawl that spoke of his Western roots, though she knew that as the child of Russian immigrants, he was fluent in that language.

Jessica didn't care what he thought of her. She'd battled for her position as head of Sterling Stops, a quick-shop chain, dismissing gossip that she'd married her second husband for his fortune. Her first husband had been the result of an impetuous teenage marriage, and from him she'd learned to stay away from very physical men—like Alexi.

In business, she knew how to fight above and below the board table. She knew how to cut short taunts and how to ignore them. In life, she knew how rough a frustrated young husband could be with a teenage bride—and yet a second, older husband could love her so much she could almost forget her desperate past, that everyday struggle to survive. "Then do. Please do. Say that you don't trust me."

"What do you want?" The question shot at her like a bullet.

Jessica tried not to shiver, but the dampness and freezing chill had seeped into her flesh. "I need your services."

A corner of his hard mouth lifted and there was a flicker of disdain in his silver eyes. "Do you?"

"Stop playing games. Are you available or not?"

This time, warmth slid into his eyes, his mouth softening just that bit. "You must be determined to go the distance in this bad weather. You're freezing, soaked through and shivering in that expensive, too-light jacket. You're expecting me to take off my coat and offer it to you, aren't you? That would be the thing for a gentleman to do, wouldn't it, Mrs. Sterling? But then, I'm only a bartender, aren't I? A man for hire?"

Those hard blue-gray eyes slid down then up her body once more. Alexi's temporary warmth shifted suddenly into a cold, hard statement. "Take off that coat. It's wet and you're freezing."

"No, thanks. I can manage."

He studied her comfortable but light leather shoes, one tiny strap torn free. "You weren't planning to come after me tonight, were you? Why did you?"

Jessica had been coming from the kitchen, carrying a filled plate to her suite; she'd intended to eat while she watched a favorite movie. Then she'd seen Alexi move down the corridor. He'd been wearing that heavy coat—how she envied him now—but her curiosity had kept her in the shadows. A man with a lover wouldn't do. Pillow talk with another woman could endanger Willow. If he was seeing a woman, involved with someone, Jessica wanted to know and she'd decided to follow him.

She should have waited. Dressed in a light sweater, lounging jacket and pants, she hadn't been prepared to do anything other than walk through the luxurious hallways to the kitchen.

Then, unexpectedly, Alexi Stepanov had swept through the hallway—tall, brooding, dangerous, and perfect to protect Willow.

He had deliberately led Jessica through a freezing night and a rough path. Her usual chignon had torn free beneath the hood and she'd impatiently ripped away the pins. Few people saw her with her hair unconfined or mussed; she resented that Alexi had studied her hair, inspecting it on his finger.

A man who caught the smallest detail, who noticed everything, was exactly what she wanted. But not this close and not her.

"I didn't expect that—no. I was hoping for a quiet corner for a discussion."

"You've got that now."

Her feet were freezing! A shiver ran through her before she could hide it.

Alexi inhaled impatiently and then his hand was at her chest, tugging down the zipper. Once free, he tugged the jacket off of her and tossed it aside.

In the next instant she was inside his coat and pressed against him. "Okay, now talk," he ordered briskly.

Panic gripped her and before she could retrieve her composure, Alexi had caught her fear, studying her.

"I'm only sharing body warmth, Mrs. Sterling," he said gently, without the sarcasm she'd expected. Those silvery eyes slid down to her throat, where she was certain her racing pulse could be seen. His voice was husky and soft. "Don't be afraid."

She'd been a teenager on her first wedding night and trapped by a man who—who wasn't her gentle second husband. Jessica pushed back the fear that could leap through the years, pursuing her if a man came too close. "I...of course I'm not. You're mistaken. I'm only a little cold."

"That admission must have cost you." Was that a little humor in those cold eyes, the slight softening of those hard lips?

Dangerous. Quick. A hunter tuned to his senses. Sleek. Powerful. Male. The words danced through her mind, but Jessica forced herself to stand rigidly within his arms, her hands at her sides.

He was looking too closely at her, invading that tight secret core she held very private and safe.

Within inches of her face, Alexi's was even harder. He was scented of soap and man, of the elements outside, of a predator circling her, setting her on edge.

Intent on relaxing in front of her suite's television set, Jessica hadn't bothered with a bra beneath her light sweater. Neither the light sweater or his black sweatshirt softened his body's hard impact against hers.

"Settle down, Mrs. Sterling," he whispered, and the rumble of his deep voice vibrated against her body.

This man knew exactly what to do with a woman in his arms. He knew how to hold, to look, how to be gentle.... Jessica forced herself to look up at him and tried to push aside her fear of a man holding her. Alexi was too close, too strong, too masculine. "I think we should confer at another time."

He lifted that black eyebrow, challenging her. "I'm a busy man. Now is good."

If she told the wrong man, she could endanger Willow, the only friend she really trusted.

The wind howled outside and, without looking, Alexi said, "It's changed back to snow. The ground will be covered soon—ice beneath the snow."

"If you knew that I wanted to talk with you, you could have made this easier."

"I wanted to know your limits—how badly you wanted me. You *do* want me, don't you, Mrs. Sterling?"

She resented the sexual inference and anger ripped at her senses. "You're toying with me. I don't like it."

"Just testing that temper, and you've got one for sure. It might keep you warm on the trip back, but you won't get a second chance at me. Simmer down."

"And just stand here? Next to you?" she demanded.

He shrugged lightly. "You have choices. If you don't want what I have to offer—leave."

"Mikhail wouldn't like for you not to help a guest in need."

His expression hardened. "Or a woman looking for—entertainment?"

* * *

Wasn't that what Heather, his ex-fiancée, had called him— "Entertainment until better things came along?"

Alexi didn't like what his senses were telling him—that Jessica Sterling was soft and fragrant and all woman. His senses told him that he liked her in his arms—that soft, curved body against his—that he wanted to taste those lush lips.

He wanted to burn away the years of abstinence, to move with her, in her, slick and hot and—

And his body was hardening, a physical reaction to her body against his—

Oh, no. Not that again. His mind flashed big warning signals at him. He'd been burned by another woman, just like this one—perfectly painted and groomed and expensive and spoiled. He'd jumped through hoops, been almost stripped of his savings and resources to please a woman like this, and past the momentary sexual gratification, there was no satisfying Heather's whims—

And he'd lost a measure of his pride, a commodity the Stepanov men held dear.

Alexi stepped back and stared at Jessica, fighting the hard throb of his body and the knowledge that women like this knew how to strip a man of everything—including his pride. He'd almost given in to that helpless, terrified look—like a little wounded bird needing help and comfort.

He'd felt the tremor of her body, her panic as he held her. That soft, female body—

With a contemptuous sidelong look, Jessica turned away, her arms tight around herself. "You really don't like me, do you?" she asked quietly, the wind's howl almost swallowing her words.

"Does it matter?" Alexi removed his coat and placed it over her shoulders. Before he could stop his hand, he reached to lift that heavy silky hair up and over the collar. His fingers crushed the strands momentarily, possessively, but he forced them open and away.

Jessica eased her arms into the sleeves and allowed him to turn her and button the coat. "Thank you," she said tightly, as if the courtesy grated. "I'll return it to you in just a moment."

He turned the collar up around her face, needing to touch her hair, her cheek, just once more. She looked like a child, huddled into his too-large coat. A very expensive, spoiled and angry child who didn't trust him.

"Let's cut to the chase, shall we?" she asked, and moved away from him, staring out into the snowflakes sliding down the window's plastic coverings.

"Are your feet cold?" he asked, while his mind prowled around why this woman would leave the warmth, security and luxury of the Amoteh Resort to follow him on a winter night as bitter and treacherous as this one.

Jessica pivoted to him, a myriad of color—reddish hair, flashing green eyes and flushed face. The emeralds on her hand glittered as she swept it out, a gesture that dismissed his question. "You need money. I have it. I need a job done and you're the first on my list to do it. My late husband always said, pick the right man for the job. I think that's you."

That grated, and Alexi leaned against the wall, folded his arms over his chest and waited. "What brings you to any conclusion about my needs?"

"You may be remodeling this now, but you're making tentative probes on property—probably to start a new life away from Wyoming. You sometimes tend bar at the Seagull's Perch...the owner is getting ready to retire. Two and two say you're looking at buying—if you can. I just might be able to help you do that."

"That's a lot of information. Did you hire someone for all that? Or did you just dig it up yourself?"

"Give me credit. I have resources and I don't like to fence. Either you're interested or you're not." She picked up a towel between her hands and studied it. As if satisfied, she sat on a low bench, kicked off her shoes and wrapped the towel around her bare feet. She chafed them briskly and watched him. "It's freezing in here. Make up your mind."

"I'm listening."

She shivered and huddled within his coat. "I haven't gotten

any assurances that you won't tell what you know, or that you will do the job."

Interesting, Alexi thought. A determined woman, not asking for relief from the cold; she stood her ground, demanding an answer. "One of us has to go first and lay something on the bargaining table. That's you. And while we're at it, I don't like people prying into my business. Tell me just what you know."

She seemed to simmer, her eyes lashing at him, her lips compressed. "Okay. I ran a search on the newspaper archives online. You bought an old ranch, started a home on it, and your engagement picture to Heather Pell wasn't followed by a wedding article. I tracked her to another marriage, quite a wealthy one, near the same wedding date as yours should have been. That must have hurt, because that was three years ago and you're still guarding yourself. I saw that at the dance last week. No friendly conversation, no polite manners past dancing that one time with me. You tended bar, giving the staff a break, danced with your cousins and their mothers, your aunt and Georgia, the cook, some guests and a few of the staff. You seemed to enjoy dancing with the woman who supplies soap for the Amoteh. Willow? Wasn't that her name?"

Jessica seemed to be watching him for a reaction to her question. A sweet, gentle and happy woman, Willow Longstreet supplied the resort with soap, fashioned like a strawberry, from her shop. The Native American word for strawberry was Amoteh, a name used by the town and several of the shops. A strawberry design was used by the resort as a logo on all its bathroom and other amenities.

Alexi had instantly liked Willow. But he decided to let Jessica take the lead, and he remained silent.

When he didn't answer, temper flashed in those green eyes. "At the dance, there was a woman hunting you, and you could have had her. Instead you snubbed her. She loved it, of course, and it only made her game more fun. But you like to do the hunting, don't you? Men like you do. They enjoy the macho role."

"You've moved past a job you wanted done into the personal lane, Red. I'd watch that."

He thought of Marcella, a frequent guest at the Amoteh and always on the lookout for a new bedroom thrill. Marcella had been chasing Jarek and Mikhail before they married, and now she'd blatantly turned her attention to Alexi. He'd had to peel her off him more than once during his stay and still she managed to waylay him.

But the woman who had moved against him just moments ago was all natural flowing softness, the kind his hands ached to cup. He could still feel her body in his arms, that tight waist, just the flare of those swaying hips—

Alexi pushed away from the wall. He was too restless with his emotions, his need to know more about the wealthy Mrs. Jessica Sterling. He watched her shiver again, that lush bottom lip quiver as if her teeth were chattering, but her eyes never left him.

"You must want me bad, lady," he said slowly, and instinctively knew those words would set her off.

Then Alexi opened the door to the living room, stepped inside and closed it behind him.

He smiled briefly, enjoying Jessica's furious expression.

She wasn't a woman to back down.

And just maybe he needed to know more about her.

Two

Jessica sat, hunched in Alexi's big, warm coat, her bare feet wrapped in a towel that provided no warmth in the chilly, gutted sunroom. Wind rattled the plastic that covered the windows and a draft lifted the tendrils beside her face.

She shivered; at two-thirty in the morning she could have been snuggled in the resort's massive bed created by Stepanov's Furniture. If she'd been unable to sleep, she could be sitting in front of her suite's blazing fire, working on the corporation business or watching her favorite old black-and-white movie. She could be in a luxurious aromatherapy bath, a rejuvenating mask on her face, and listening to relaxing music.

Alexi Stepanov had tugged her against him, held her easily. An irritating, arrogant—

Jessica rubbed her bare toes with both hands, willing warmth into them. If she left now, she might not get him to help protect Willow.

She inhaled the scent of freshly cut wood. The flapping of the plastic on the windows irritated her, just like the man. A draft on the floor stirred sawdust that had been swept into a pile; bits of it tumbled across the rough board floor toward her.

She stood abruptly, slipped into her wet shoes and grabbed her jacket, then she pushed open the door Alexi had just entered. "I'm not through with you—"

"Shut the door." Alexi was crouched in front of a woodstove, adding kindling to a growing flame. The new stovepipe said it had been recently installed. Alexi glanced at her as he added a chunk of wood from an old galvanized tub.

She'd taken baths in a tub just like that back in rural Arkansas....

Jessica studied the rough but large room, the large windows facing the Pacific Ocean. An electric skillet, toaster and coffeemaker sat on a door, propped between two sawhorses. A wooden deck chair, walnut in a sturdy design typical of Fadey Stepanov's furniture, sat in front of the windows; hand-loomed cushions matched the dark brown and maroon blanket thrown over the back. Jessica stared at the massive walnut bed, covered with a down blanket in dark green with crimson strips, a very masculine design. A square of commercial beige carpet covered the floor. A battery lantern sat next to a stack of magazines on a gleaming, chunky table. Resting on a wooden box, a battered suitcase held neatly folded clothing. More folded clothing was in a laundry basket on the floor. A mirror hung on the wall over another table. An enamel basin with soap and neatly folded towels rested on it.

Alexi had deliberately drawn her into a bald confrontation, preventing an easy retreat. He had played the game, set the rules and had won. Her temper rising, Jessica slammed the door.

She struggled to push down that passionate, fighting side of her that few people had experienced. The fire blazed now and Alexi turned to walk toward a small kitchen table with two wooden chairs. He poured coffee from a thermos into a mug marked with the Amoteh Resort's strawberry logo. He sipped the steaming brew slowly and watched her.

Water dripped steadily from the ceiling, plopping into two buckets, and the fire crackled while Jessica struggled to retain her composure and the image she wanted to project—the businesswoman making deals. She inhaled slowly; she'd handled problem people before.

"You're playing games. I do not like games, or surprises. We could have talked in here," Jessica said tightly, finishing the static silence that scratched her nerves like fingernails on a blackboard. "And I do *not* want you badly."

"Are your feet cold?" he asked casually, and that easy drawl set her temper climbing again.

"Of course they are. You made me follow you through ice and snow. Talk—if that's what you call it—in a freezing room when all the while we could have talked where it is warm— and *I do not want you badly.*"

He poured another cup of coffee and lifted it. "Come and get it, Mrs. Sterling."

She tensed, weighing his "Come and get it." Was that a sexual invitation? Or a challenge to start a war?

"This is from the Amoteh. They make better coffee than I do." The man was unreadable, his eyes cool upon her, slits of silver between those heavy black lashes, shadowed by his brows.

Her senses told her that there was a savage ruthlessness about this man that only a few had seen. If he decided to help protect Willow, and if whoever was bothering her was capable of physical violence, Alexi's primitive instinct would be needed.

Jessica hesitated on a heartbeat, then walked to him, taking the metal cup. "Thank you."

"That must have cost you," he murmured, and humor lit those silvery eyes.

She turned and walked to the stove. The hot coffee warmed her slightly, and she kicked off her shoes, placing them near the fire to dry. Without turning, she stared at the fire in the stove's open door and sipped the coffee. A soft blow hit her back and a ball of heavy workmen's socks bounced at her feet. "Put those on."

She turned to find Alexi seated in one of the wooden chairs, which had been turned toward the fire. He stripped off his work boots and sprawled backward, long legs outstretched. A mug of coffee rested on his flat stomach, his eyes slits of silver in his hard, shadowed face.

Irritated by his cool testing of her, Jessica spoke slowly. She wanted him to know exactly what she thought of him. "There's a curse on Amoteh, placed on it by Kamakani, that Hawaiian chieftain captured and enslaved by whalers in another century. He died on Strawberry Hill, not far from here, cursing this place. I truly believe you might be a part of that curse, Mr. Stepanov. At least for me. And I know that it's said that his curse can only be lifted by a woman who knows her own heart, dancing in front of his grave…. Don't count on any dancing from me, Stepanov. Play any more games with me and you're in for your own curse."

He lifted his mug in a toast and nodded, acknowledging her accusation.

"This is what you're really like, isn't it? Not the easygoing guy everyone thinks you are. This…this retreat is where you come to be as you really are—dark, moody, deliberately obtuse and difficult."

"And you want me."

The statement, driven home once again, irritated; just that slightly foreign inflection had slipped into Alexi's deep Western drawl, just the nip to remind her that Alexi's father, mother and uncles had emigrated from Russia.

At the dance, Alexi with his cousins, Jarek and Mikhail, had circulated in the filled ballroom, obviously enjoying their family, the guests and friends of the close-knit community. Tall, dark, almost sleek, despite rugged looks and broad shoulders, they'd caused more than one woman to stare.

Jarek and Mikhail had held their wives close and tender, loving intimacy flowing between them with a touch, a look.

"That's Alexi, their cousin," Willow had whispered to Jessica. "He's unmarried and gorgeous. He's sweet, too. I dare you to dance with him."

"You're on," Jessica had said, and had moved toward Alexi. While dancing with him, she had not sensed "sweet," only brooding and dangerous.

And Willow might need that.

Jessica decided to skip negotiations and go straight for what she wanted. While framing her negotiation package, she scooped to pick up the ball of socks and went to sit on the cot, placing her coffee on the table beside it. She jammed on the socks, rolled the extra length into thick cuffs and, as an afterthought, stood and removed the shearling coat. She arranged her damp light jacket over the cord stretched near the stove. Jessica walked back to his sprawling bed, determined to regain her poise and have her say with Mr. Alexi Stepanov.

Alexi watched that sensual, gliding walk, elegant even with the large heavy socks rolled upon her feet. He could have told her that her light tan sweater did nothing to hide the peaks of her nipples, but he wouldn't.

He wouldn't let her know that earlier, that softness had caused his hands to open possessively upon the coat over her back. That her curves had branded his body with an unwanted need. That the scent of her caused him to want to nuzzle her hair, to feel that silkiness against his skin. That the need to taste her lips had almost driven him to—

That stir of sensual interest irritated Alexi, the ramrod-straight way she'd marched back to the bed and plopped herself onto it—all that soft flesh beneath her clothing had bounced and quivered as she settled in to stare at him coldly. As if she were sitting at the head of a corporate boardroom table, Jessica Sterling had crossed her long, sleek legs that disappeared into his overlarge socks and stared at him.

She pushed a thick wave back from her cheek and inhaled, which served to push her breasts against that thin sweater.

Alexi inhaled sharply; that sweater seemed to have nothing beneath it but creamy soft curves. When she crossed her arms and looked at him, her breasts lifted and bulged against the material.

His body had locked on to several facts at once: a very sensuous woman was sitting on his bed, he hadn't been sexually aroused in a long time, and Jessica Sterling—rich, determined, selfish, spoiled—was definitely not the woman he wanted to arouse him.

"I have a friend whom I think is in trouble. I want you to investigate and take care of whomever is troubling her—quietly. If the police are called in, that person could go underground easily, only to surface when least expected. I prefer to keep my friend out of any problems. She's really sweet and kind, and—and I want her protected. I want whatever is bothering her to be—removed discreetly. My friend lives here in Amoteh."

Alexi frowned slightly; as a Stepanov male, his protective instincts had raised instantly. "Tell me who she is."

"You've met her—Willow Longstreet. She makes soap with the Amoteh strawberry logo for the resort? She has a shop on the street by the waterfront—Willow's Soaps? You danced with her?"

Alexi tipped back on his chair, rocking slightly on the back two legs. Willow had worn arty, flowing clothes, her head covered with black curling hair cut in a bob with a center part. Her tiny glasses were usually at the end of her nose. At the dance, Willow had seemed open and happy, delighted to be with her friends, and he'd enjoyed her company.

The women seemed unlikely friends; Willow's open warmth contrasted with Jessica Sterling's cool, sleek, almost hard businesslike persona.

Yet she cared enough to investigate a man who might protect her friend. Alexi suspected that Jessica hid many secrets about herself, including that fine edge of her temper.

He resented his need to nudge that temper and reveal the woman she hid....

Jessica stood and went to stare at the fire in the grate. Her voice was soft and reflective. "I don't want anything to happen to her—Willow is special. Just name your price and protect her. But don't let her know—and don't...don't get involved with her. You're not a match. I'll pay whatever you want. Just take care of whomever is bothering her. She won't tell me exactly what's happening, but several incidents have happened that I think indicate someone is threatening her. And she's distracted. Something is very wrong. She's innocent and men like you—I can handle someone as difficult as you, but she's—*Do not get romantically involved with her, and that's an order—''*

The ringing of a cell phone caused Jessica to stop; she impatiently reached for her jacket, taking a tiny upscale phone from her pocket. She answered in a curt businesslike tone. ''Sterling.''

She frowned and turned from Alexi, then walked to the huge windows facing the ocean and spoke quietly, ''Howard, I told you not to call me.''

After a silence Jessica said, ''Don't you dare come here. I am on personal leave that has nothing to do with the corporation. I am only to be reached for business emergencies, not because you are lonesome. You have a wife, remember?''

Alexi stared at the crackling fire. It wasn't his business if Jessica Sterling had impatient lovers—

''Don't you dare speak to me that way. I loved your father very much and Robert married me because he loved me. And you are nothing like him. It's only been two years since he passed away and I think about him every day…. Listen, Howard, I was not…*am* not a trophy wife. Robert taught me how to run the company and I'm doing it. Don't call back… Don't you threaten me, Howard.''

Alexi frowned. Jessica's husband was reportedly twice her age and ''Junior'' was old enough to have a wife. He seemed to want Jessica. She didn't want to play and some jerk was trying to bully her— Impatiently, Alexi stood, walked to Jessica and took the cell phone from her.

''You heard the lady. Stop calling her. She's with me…. I am Alexi Stepanov,'' he said into the phone. He didn't wait for the man sputtering at the other end of the line to recover before turning off the phone. Alexi handed it back to her—her eyes were wide and stunned, and he raised his fingertip to her chin, lifted slightly to close her slightly parted lips.

At that moment she looked young and unguarded and sweet. It seemed only right to follow his instincts and nuzzle her cheek with his, to then inhale the delicate floral and rain scent of her hair.

She stood tensed and still. The air around her seemed to

quiver delicately, fascinating him, and Alexi could not resist brushing his lips across hers.

The slight lifting of her lips, the trembling response that he'd sensed rather than felt, ricocheted inside Alexi, his need to kiss her vibrating within him.

Innocent, his senses warned as color started to move up those smooth, creamy cheeks.

The air seemed to quiver, shifting and changing around Jessica again, and Alexi tuned into what he felt coming from her— awareness of him as a man...and fear.

Someone had hurt her.

As a Stepanov male, Alexi brooded about men who would hurt women. Was it the man who had just called?

"I turned my cell phone off while following you. I have to leave it on for business purposes in case I'm needed," she said furiously, and punched the On button.

When the cell phone rang furiously in her hand, Alexi said quietly, "If you want to talk with me, turn that thing off. You have choices. Make them."

Alexi wasn't sparing time on a married man harassing a woman who didn't want him. As though she disliked taking orders, Jessica's green eyes narrowed up at him and she stepped a few feet away. Without looking at the cell phone, she punched a button and placed the unit on the table. "It's off. You're arrogant, Mr. Stepanov."

"Thank you."

"That wasn't a compliment. I handle my own affairs. It's Willow who needs your protection and help. I'm willing to pay for that service."

Alexi weighed Jessica's proposal. This woman asked nothing for herself and resented his interference in her life.

Jessica walked around the room, clearly keeping her distance from him. Those sidelong glances said she was mentally circling him. "Will you see to Willow's safety? I want an answer. Now. I'm ready to negotiate a price."

"There is no answer yet. I'll want to talk with Willow." Concentrating on her offer was difficult when the firelight outlined those lush curves and she stood in front of his bed, and his mind was picturing all those soft, pale curves lying in his arms—

Suddenly too warm, Alexi impatiently removed his sweatshirt and tossed it aside. He opened a door onto a remodeled wooden deck facing the ocean and stepped out into the snow. He focused on letting his skin—and his hard, pounding sexual desire cool.

He frowned when the door scraped and Jessica stood at his side, overlooking the ocean. "You can't run away from me, Mr. Stepanov. I want an answer."

"Get inside." His voice was too rough, his control slipping.

She didn't move or speak, but stood at his side.

Jessica might be wealthy and spoiled, but she wanted her friend protected.

He sensed that she would stand, stubbornly freezing, before moving. "I'm cold," he said softly. "Let's go inside."

He turned, placed one arm around her and drew her to his side. With his other hand, he opened the door to his living quarters. Jessica resisted his light touch directing her inside momentarily, then she lifted her head and walked into the room.

He'd allowed his hand to open on that neat waist, to fit just slightly onto the curve of her hip. He resented the instinctive hardening of his body, the need burning low in his gut. *But she felt so right, soft and feminine.... And for him, sex was a long time ago...he simply wanted to take her and lose himself in her...to forget another woman....*

His hunger was natural, considering his abstinence for over three years. No woman had seemed right—until now. With the door closed, Jessica moved toward the fire, her arms crossed.

Drops of water glistened in her hair, beautiful against the dark reddish tones highlighted by the firelight. She seemed deep in thought, and then she turned suddenly to study him. Those eyes were dark and mysterious, tracing his body down, then upward. His jeans were already tight across his hips. "Do you always arouse so easily, Mr. Stepanov?"

She had felt what ran between them and had met the problem immediately. No flirtation, no games, just facts. Alexi smiled;

Mrs. Sterling was getting more interesting all the time. "No. But it has been a long time for me, and you are here, very close, in my home."

"You should take care of your problem—somehow, before talking with Willow." The order came soft and guarded, and she turned away suddenly, but not before he caught the flush moving up her cheeks, the downward shy look, avoiding his.

"Did the man who called you…was he the one who hurt you?"

Her defenses shot up, those green eyes flashing. Magnificent, Alexi thought, fierce, proud, loyal, protective, passionate in her anger. Her veneer had been breached and the woman beneath it fascinated him.

"We're negotiating a business deal here, Stepanov. There is no reason to get into my personal profile, other than—please do not go to Willow in that…that condition."

Now Alexi was amused, enjoying playing with her, teasing her even more. All the little colorful pieces inside her seemed to shift, presenting the woman he wanted to know better, and one she wanted to hide.

"It happens," he said, diving straight for the woman beneath that polished surface. "You're a woman. I'm a man. I can sense an excitement in you, a scent. It triggers a natural response…. Willow seems like an understanding, helpful woman," he added, just to stir Jessica once more.

"Willow is wonderful and an innocent. Just do what men do to relieve whatever—"

"And just what do men do?"

She waved her hand airily and the emeralds on it sparkled, reminding him that she had been married—married, and still shy of a man in close quarters. "You know. Whatever men do. Get a magazine or watch a movie—or find some woman—but not Willow."

"Don't you think that Willow would want to choose for herself what she wants?"

"No. Not in this instance," she stated curtly.

He had to come closer, to catch every nuance of her expression. "Why not me? What is wrong with me?"

She bit her lip and studied the overlong socks on her feet. "Well," she stated briskly as her toes wiggled within the socks. "You're potent. And I suppose if you tried, you could charm the pants off Willow in a very short time. She's just not up to you. You have the advantage, and that just isn't fair, is it?"

Jessica knew how to speak clearly to men, defining just what she wanted, defining the rules.

Alexi had never been good at following rules.

"And you are? Up to me?" He wondered what those pale, slender feet would feel like against his own, rubbing her insole up and down his calf while he buried himself in her—

She frowned fiercely up at him and laid out the facts like bullets shooting at him. "I'm wealthy and single. Men want me. They don't get me. You may be a sex magnet, but *don't you dare play with Willow.*"

He'd found the live heat she hid inside that veneer and went for it again. "It is possible that she might not be able to resist me. After all, you have said that I am potent, have you not? What is this 'potent'? As a man? As a conversationalist? How do you define—"

Jessica stood; her hand lifted and her finger tapped his bare chest with each word. *"Leave Willow alone—that way."*

Alexi didn't miss the light sweep of her hand across his chest to his shoulder, that little tremble before it lifted. He wanted her hands on him—everywhere. *Without the brand of another man's ring.*

To keep himself from reaching for her, Alexi stepped back and crouched to feed the stove with wood and carefully bank it for the hours that remained until morning.

His hands needed to be busy, because they ached to touch this woman, to claim her. He closed the door as firmly as he wanted his sensual interest in this woman to die. "We have talked enough," he stated, recognizing his accent in the husky words. "Please make yourself comfortable in my home. Or you may leave, though I advise against it. Morning will be here in a few hours. I will speak to Willow tomorrow. Then I will give my decision to you."

* * *

Jessica watched Alexi yawn and stretch, and his hands went
to his jeans' snap. His eyebrows lifted, his eyes silvery beneath
his heavy lashes. "You may turn away or you may watch."

She turned quickly, heat moving up her throat. She never
blushed, and yet Alexi drew something from her—"I'm leaving."

His body pressed lightly against her back and then his cheek
was against hers. He nuzzled aside her hair and whispered in
her ear, "If you do, I shall have to follow you in the cold,
making certain that you are safe. Here, we are warm and
safe.... You have just trembled. Why are you nervous of me?
Because I have been obviously aroused?"

"I don't know why, but you like to torment me, Mr. Stepanov."

"Of course. Because you are so delightful to watch. All that
fire leaps to life so easily." His smile curved along her cheek.
"You are hot now. I think you are blushing. I like that—that
you react to me. Do you think it's true? That women think of
me as a sex magnet?"

"Jerk."

Jessica hadn't been teased in her lifetime, and Alexi Stepanov was unrelenting. A moment later he said, "My jeans are
off and I'm in my bed. You may turn around now."

"Jerk," she repeated as she walked toward the window to
study the storm outside and a slash of sleet hit the glass. Jessica
weighed that half-mile back to the resort and the longer walk
to Willow's shop and apartment. But then how could Jessica
explain to Willow why she was out walking at three o'clock
in the morning?

Jessica turned back to Alexi, whose bare back above the
blankets—those warm, heavy blankets—was turned to her. His
skin gleamed, covering a wide expanse of muscles.

With a sigh loud enough for him to hear, she pushed and
shoved the heavy lawn chair closer to the stove. She settled
into the chair and briskly wrapped the softly woven gray-green
throw over her. She breathed Alexi's scent—masculine, soap,
smoke, and dark with layers. First came arrogance, a man who

liked control and setting his terms. Then, he'd obviously been wounded in the past, his pride showing when his ex-fiancée was mentioned. Protective? Too much for an independent woman, especially when he took away the cell phone, dismissing Howard.

Alexi liked to torment her. Why? Definitely sensual, he'd picked up on her awareness of him—who wouldn't be aware of a man like that, all of six foot three and in lean, perfect condition, almost animalistic grace? Snuggling down into the soft crocheted throw, Jessica brooded about the man who was apparently asleep and very comfortable.

Jessica shifted on the chair and pulled the throw up to her chin. "'Body warmth,'" she muttered. Alexi had wanted to hold her against him, gauge her, study her. He'd promptly dismissed any courtesy between them.

She glanced at him and let the warmth of the fire sink into her flesh. Alexi was determined to make her play his game. Jessica preferred to play her own.

She threw back the throw and came to her feet. She crossed the length of the room quickly and jabbed a finger against his shoulder. He grunted and Jessica tapped his shoulder. "Hey. Wake up. I'm not done talking to you."

"I need sleep," Alexi said drowsily. "You are a pest, I think."

"I can be your nightmare, bud—"

Alexi moved too quickly, grabbing her wrist and holding it as he turned. He scowled at her. "You can sleep tomorrow. I work. I wouldn't advise you to irritate me more, not if you want me to help Willow."

"I said I'd pay you."

"With you, everything comes with a bill, right? Money solves everything?"

"It doesn't hurt."

Those icy, silver eyes searched her face. "Right," he said, turning her hand to glance at her heavy set of emerald wedding rings. "Everything costs something, doesn't it?"

His bitter tone cut at her, the reason she had married and had sold herself. "You—"

With a tug Alexi brought her down to the bed and, before she could scramble free, Alexi leaned over her, his forearms braced beside her. "You are exhausted, and pushing to get what you want. I do not like to be pushed, especially by a woman who is used to getting her way—and can buy what she wants. Go to sleep now."

Muscles bunched beneath that gleaming skin, his shoulders blocking out the room, his expression fierce and close—and there was too much of him, pressed too close, even with the layers of cloth between their bodies. Her hands were open on his chest, the textures and the warmth there, burning her palms. Beneath her fingers, powerful muscles slid and tensed.

Jessica couldn't move, her body trembling. As he had when he'd tugged her into his coat, Alexi had moved very quickly. Her mind flashed with images of another man, in another time, holding her against her will, hurting her. She pushed hard against his chest. "Get...away...from me," she ordered.

With a low growl and a look of disgust, Alexi flipped the blanket over her and turned his back. Jessica rolled to her feet, looked down at him and hated him at that moment. She jerked the blanket from the bed, bunched it and hauled it back to the wooden chair. She settled into the chair and briskly arranged the blanket and throw around her. Jessica looked at the pillow beneath Alexi's head and was on her feet once more.

At the bed, she latched both hands onto the pillow and began pulling it from him. Without turning, he held it tight.

"You're not very hospitable, Mr. Stepanov."

"No, I am not. You are a difficult woman and you are costing me sleep."

"Let me have this pillow."

Alexi lifted his head and Jessica jammed the pillow beneath her arm as she walked back to her chair.

The next three hours were going to be very long.... "I'm not done with you yet, Mr. Arrogant Macho Stepanov. Otherwise, I'd already be walking back. You've made your opinion of me pretty clear, and I don't like it. I still haven't given you mine. Expect that in the morning."

"There's more? I can't wait."

* * *

Alexi turned to study the woman sleeping in the sturdy wooden lawn chair. Blue shadows rested beneath her eyes, her hand bracing her head at an odd angle.

With a resigned sigh, he eased from the bed and walked to her. Bundled in his blankets, Jessica was the perfect unwanted female invader.

Whatever man she didn't want to accept, the married man, would probably soon be coming to press her—and because Alexi had given his name, he would be involved. His impression of Jessica Sterling had been correct—she was big trouble.

Alexi skimmed his hand lightly over her hair and its warm fire lit something he had guarded for years.

He jerked his hand back, freeing it from the lure of that silky, fragrant hair. Tenderness for this female shark wouldn't do, and a sexual encounter wouldn't be simple.

"Alexi..." she whispered in her sleep, and the drowsy sound locked his bare feet to the floor. "I need you..."

He closed his mind against the sensual need rocketing through his body, but it throbbed on, ignoring his wishes. Her breast lay over a heavy fold of the blanket and his hand ached to cup that perfect softness.

Bracing himself against that dangerous need, Alexi bent and eased Jessica, complete with pillow and blanket, into his arms.

She snuggled against his chest, rubbing her cheek against his shoulder, and Alexi didn't move, forcing his breath to slow. With her defenses down, Jessica looked young and sweet and innocent.

An involvement with this woman would only bring frustration and pain.

He studied that pale face, where the chestnut strands flowed across her cheek and onto his shoulder, a fragile silky web joining their bodies—

Alexi's indrawn breath hissed in the silence of the room. Wanting to rid himself of the danger of this woman, Alexi carried her back to his bed, lowered her slightly and let her fall the last inch. He did not want to touch her in his bed.

He could not touch her; his sexual need ran too fiercely, primitively, through him.

He stood, hands on hips, looking down at the woman who was cuddling his pillow. Her hair spilled waves across the white pillowcase as she turned on her side. "Alexi..." she murmured softly, and drew the pillow down beneath the blanket.

Alexi frowned as, beneath the heavy blanket, her legs moved as if accepting the pillow, cradling it.

He'd begun to perspire, his body rock-hard.

Alexi clenched his fists and closed his eyes, shaking his head. He jerked on his jeans and pulled on a sweatshirt and socks. He sat in the chair and brooded about the curse of Chief Kamakani over Amoteh.

Because it was surely the chieftain's curse that had brought Jessica Sterling anywhere near Alexi.

Three

───

Jessica awoke to the sound of male voices arguing.

She preferred to sleep late and the Amoteh's housekeeping staff shouldn't be in her suite—

"No. You are not coming in," a man stated sharply from somewhere outside her room.

Jessica recognized that deep voice, the command and the slight accent wrapped in it. Alexi Stepanov!

She opened her eyes to a slice of brilliant sunlight and closed them as she realized she was in Alexi's bed!

She struggled against the heavy weight of the blankets tangled around her and promptly slid onto the floor. She sat, huddled in the blankets, listening to the male voices outside the comfortably warm room.

Jessica clutched the pillow against her. Alexi's scent—dark, brooding, male—wafted around her.

Alexi—arrogant, disdainful of her—sexy, aroused....

She slid up her sweater sleeve to reveal her watch; the emerald-encrusted designer timepiece read eight o'clock. Jessica braced herself for the first wave of frustration—an early riser, she was usually at her desk by this time. But then, Alexi wasn't making her life easy. He needed a lesson in handling business and keeping it out of the sensual lane.

Jessica pushed the pillow away and scrambled to her feet. She was still wearing one of his socks and bent to tug it away.

Another man's voice rumbled with just that tinge of accent. "Why can't we come in? It's cold out here. We only want to warm up before heading back for Mom's blueberry pancakes. We're supposed to unload this truckload of lumber and bring you back for a family breakfast."

Alexi's reply was hurried. "Let's unload it now. I'm hungry."

Jessica recognized Mikhail's voice. "You'll need a coat, Alexi. It's freezing out there."

"I'm fine. Please thank your parents, but I have work to do. I will see Aunt Mary Jo later and help Uncle Fadey load that order of furniture in the shipping van."

"Alexi, you just woke up. You don't have on your boots, and you look like you had a bad night. If you're sick, we can unload that lumber and you can go back to bed."

"Yes. I have a cold. Please go. No, I do not need soup. I have aspirin."

"Jarek, we're in trouble. If Mom knows that Alexi is sick because he's staying here and not at their house, she won't be happy," Mikhail said thoughtfully as if Alexi wasn't there. "We've got to get him to the house—now."

"You're not moving me. I am fine where I am."

"Oh, no?" the other two male voices challenged.

Jessica smiled coldly. Alexi clearly did not want the men inside his living quarters. He wanted to hide her, did he?

After last night, after Alexi had deliberately drawn her out into the weather, had treated her so arrogantly—*and put her in his bed without her permission*—Jessica intended Alexi to have a very bad day. He would either help root out whomever was causing Willow fear and distress, or he wouldn't. But Alexi would pay for tormenting Jessica.

She walked to the line where her jacket hung and drew it on, firmly zipping it to her throat. She slipped into her ruined shoes and lamented their destruction, due to Alexi drawing her into his lair. Whatever she did to him today, he deserved. She tore away the damaged strap with a temper that she pushed down as she smoothed her clothing and her hair.

Jessica picked up Alexi's boots and his coat and the leather work gloves she found on the table, and walked to the door.

She opened it slowly to the three tall men standing in the cluttered, cold sunroom. "Hi," she said softly, drowsily, and hoped she sounded as if she'd just come from Alexi's bed—which she had. She eased around Alexi, who was blocking the doorway and her stage entrance to make his life hell—at least for a short time.

Obviously, Alexi did not want his cousins to know that Jessica had stayed the night. What he didn't want was perfect to expose...

Jarek and Mikhail Stepanov, in heavy jackets and work clothes stared at her—then at Alexi.

Jessica faked a drowsy yawn and batted her lashes innocently up at Alexi. Beneath his eyebrows, and the frown line between them, his blue eyes narrowed. His lips pressed firmly, angrily, in that dark, stubble-covered jaw.

"Good morning, Alexi," she murmured in an intimate lovers'-morning-after tone.

Mikhail's body stiffened, but the quick movement of his lips was a smile, soon hidden. While Alexi stood, silent and forbidding, Mikhail nodded formally. "Good morning, Jessica."

Jarek grinned widely. "Yes, good morning."

Jessica walked to Alexi and thoroughly enjoyed his fierce scowl. "Here you go," she said lightly, and dropped the boots intentionally close to his sock-covered feet. She handed the jacket and gloves to him, then yawned and stretched. "Did I hear something mentioned about breakfast?"

The quick narrowing of Alexi's eyes was meant to warn, so was the slapping of the leather gloves against his hand. Instead she took the gestures as a challenge.

"You are not invited, Mrs. Sterling," he said carefully.

"Oh, I'm disappointed. I was hoping to spend more time with you." She feigned an apologetic half smile and batted her lashes at him again, enjoying the waves of frustration and anger coming from Alexi. He would learn not to play games with her. "It was rude of me to invite myself."

"Not rude at all. Our parents would love to have you," Mikhail said briskly.

"Are you certain? Oh, that would be lovely. I would just be a minute freshening up, and I do need to make the bed." Jessica looked up at Alexi. "But Alexi doesn't want—"

"He'll feel better after he eats," Jarek stated and, with a chuckle, stepped outside the door. With a brisk nod, Mikhail followed.

Alexi jammed on his boots, laced them furiously and jerked on his coat, buttoning it. He scowled down at her, a muscle in his jaw clenching. "Now see what you have done. They think we are involved. You come out of my room, looking all soft and warm and—and you know exactly what picture you presented—as if we had spent the night making love. My family and friends have been trying to set me up with women for years. I have finally managed some peace, and now you tear it away. Once you move on, I will be left to deal with a steady flow of women wanting husbands—or lovers."

His desperation was perfect—she'd truly scored. "You're so arrogant. I suppose you think you are in demand, huh, Mr. Sex Magnet?" she taunted, serving his earlier label back at him.

"It would appear so. *You* want me, do you not?"

Jessica tilted her head and refused to be baited. "When you're emotional, your accent slips out."

"I am never emotional," Alexi stated firmly.

"Tell that to someone else. I've seen you at your worst." Jessica smiled coldly and crossed her arms. "You called this game, Stepanov. I'm just playing it. You're not exactly a sweetheart, and neither am I. I offered you a business deal. You haven't given me an answer yet. But you will."

He scowled down at her, his fist wrapping in her jacket to draw her up to his face. "You do not play with me," he ordered, spacing the words.

"I want you to take care of Willow. Will you, and how much—or won't you?"

"Who is Howard?"

She hadn't expected the harsh question. "Someone I know."

"A married man who is pursuing you, just as you want."

"I never encouraged Howard. He's my husband's son, and he's in an open marriage. Just because my husband—and I loved Robert—passed away, I'm not up for grabs." Howard had started "pursuing" her the minute that he knew his father, Robert, was interested in Jessica. When Robert and Jessica had married, Howard had been bitter, an unseated heir to the chain of Sterling Stops. As Robert's terminal illness had progressed, he'd put Jessica at the head of the company, rather than his self-serving son.

Enraged, Howard had begun to battle her on two fronts, business and personal. When she dealt with him, Jessica was always very careful to consider that her husband had dearly loved his only son. She kept Howard involved in a minor position in Sterling Stops and monitored his work herself. He was overpaid for the position, ineffective and disinterested. As executrix of her husband's estate, Jessica also monitored monthly payments to Howard and he resented her holding "Dad's purse strings."

Remembering how Alexi had interfered with Howard's call last night, Jessica said, "And I don't need anyone's protection—or interference. I handle my own business."

Alexi leveled a determined look at her. "I will not be your 'business.' You are to clear up any misconceptions immediately."

"You should have thought of that before you made me ruin these shoes." She allowed herself a smirk. "Can't you handle it, bud?"

With a low, feral growl, he leaned closer. "I tell you again— do not play games with me."

His forearm brushed her breast and Alexi inhaled sharply, pushing her away. His stare ripped from her face down to her breasts, and for just a moment, sensuality quivered between them. Then his hard blue eyes locked with hers. "Keep that jacket on."

"Orders? I don't like that. I give them, Stepanov, not take them."

When Alexi stormed out of the workroom, Jessica allowed herself a shaky but triumphant smile. He would do the job she asked, or she would make his life a living hell—and she thought she just might enjoy that.

Jessica studied herself in Alexi's shaving mirror. Her carefully applied cosmetics, her everyday protective shield behind which she ran a huge corporation, were gone—only the remains of her mascara lay smudged beneath her eyes. With a deep breath she looked at her choices from the table beneath the mirror. Willow's unscented but luxurious soap and a clean washcloth revealed the woman Jessica protected—an almost pixie-ish face with huge green eyes framed by dark brown lashes, a brief bit of a nose, high cheekbones and full lips that she carefully tried to diminish.

She used Alexi's brush carefully, drawing back her long hair into a rubber band to create a ponytail.

She looked like little more than a shiny-faced, scrubbed-clean teenager, with all the gloss and polish she had learned to protect herself placed aside. "Game time," she said quietly, determined to finish what Alexi had started.

Jessica studied herself in the mirror. "He could have given me a simple answer, and he didn't. I wasted a lot of time and energy checking him out. He is the best man for the job, but if he wants a difficult game, I know how to play. Now, let's just see what he's got."

She stepped out onto the porch and shaded her eyes against the brilliant daylight ricocheting off the snow. Fresh lumber had been stacked against the house and three tall men, with evident family resemblances, stood waiting.

Jarek and Mikhail nodded and walked toward the huge flat-bed lumber truck.

Alexi put his hands on his hips and stared coldly at her. When she came to stand in front of him, he looked down at the sweatshirt she had placed over her light jacket. That flare of his nostrils told her that she'd scored another hit to his temper by wearing his clothes. He glared at her, then down to her shoes. "I must carry you," he stated resentfully.

"Hey, I've got two feet," she answered cheerfully. "I can walk. I take care of myself."

"I never believed in that Hawaiian's curse, and now I do," Alexi stated darkly. Then, carefully and with a hint of hope, he offered, "I could carry you to the resort. Or while you wait here, I could get different shoes for you and you could walk back. This has gone far enough."

She smiled brilliantly, thoroughly enjoying his discomfort. "I've opened the gate. Let the hordes of man-hungry women begin chasing you. I wouldn't miss this for the world."

Alexi shook his head and closed his eyes as if wishing her far, far away. Then he bent and placed her over his shoulder, carrying her toward the truck. "You will keep that jacket zipped," he ordered again.

Jessica braced her hands on his taut backside to keep from flopping and to retain some small part of her dignity. *Buddy, you asked for it,* she thought, and tried for an innocent tone as she asked, "But what if I get hot? I'll have to take it off then, won't I?"

She wouldn't, of course, because without her minimizer bra, she was full-figured, and that didn't suit the sleek business image she wanted to project. But Alexi didn't know to what lengths she would go to embarrass him. At the moment, even being carried over his shoulder, Jessica knew she had the advantage.

His body tensed, but he didn't speak.

Alexi briskly lifted her up to Mikhail who was seated in the middle of the truck; Jarek sat behind the steering wheel. Before Jessica could sit, Alexi had slid up to the seat and had tugged her onto his lap.

"I've just met Alexi and he's helping me with a problem," Jessica said when the Stepanovs were all seated around Mary Jo and Fadey's long, sturdy kitchen table.

Alexi concentrated on the blueberry pancakes in front of him and tried to ignore Jessica's scent. He tried to forget the way she had sat very stiffly on his lap, the blush rising up her cheeks.

His hard arousal had been painful, the warm softness of her hips riding him over the bumpy road to the Stepanovs'. Her sharp look down at him said Jessica was feeling that sturdy sexual pressure, with only layers of cloth between the warm entrance of her body—

The sight of his oversize sweatshirt on Jessica's body had shaken him.

He wanted that emerald wedding ring off her finger, and her wearing the mark of his possession.

Alexi had partially rolled down the window despite the chill, needing fresh air to cool him. She had placed her hand on the top of the window's glass, as if she, too, needed cooling. The huge set of emerald wedding rings had caught the light, shooting sparks and questions at him:

Why should he care about a rich widow wearing another man's rings?

Why should he care that she asked nothing for herself, but for a friend?

Why did he want more than anything to take her to his bed and make love to her and forget about everything else?

Without ceremony, Alexi had carried her in his arms to the Stepanov house, a huge, jutting wooden-and-stone affair overlooking the Pacific Ocean. He had nodded to Fadey, his uncle, at the open doorway. Easing Jessica's body carefully aside, Alexi had carried her into the spacious home.

For a moment Alexi had held Jessica in his arms. He didn't want to release her; his instincts said she was his, her eyes wide and green as new leaves upon him as if a stunning emotion ran through her. "Put me down," she had whispered unevenly.

But her hand had remained on his nape, her fingers slightly digging into his skin.

In that heartbeat Alexi had known they both recognized the danger of the other.

"Put me down," she had whispered again, more urgently.

"When I am ready."

She had glanced at the Stepanov family who was evidently

enjoying the whispered exchange. "You are creating a scene, Stepanov."

"Am I? Tell me that you did not create one earlier."

Jessica had been the first to move out of their private battle arena. She had smiled at Fadey and extended her hand to shake his. "You must be Fadey Stepanov. I've heard so much about you. I love your furniture."

Fadey nodded, kissed the back of her hand and said formally, "Thank you. You are most welcome to my home."

Alexi had stared at Jarek and Mikhail, who were removing their coats and wearing the same knowing grin as Fadey. It said that they knew Alexi had finally found a woman who tested him, who fascinated him.

With a quick movement Alexi had deposited Jessica on the gleaming wooden floor. He had shrugged off his coat and had walked away, dismissing her. He didn't like the idea that Jessica had reversed the game between them, that now she held the upper hand. He had the uncomfortable feeling that he was fleeing into the safety of his aunt's large, homey kitchen.

He sipped his coffee too quickly and it burned his lip, and Jessica was dangerous. And meddlesome. And sensual. He hadn't liked the soft feel of Jessica in his arms. The way her arm had rested lightly on his shoulders—which brought those soft unbound breasts against his chest. He hadn't liked the fresh air bearing her scent—exotic yet fresh and sweet.

He chewed his aunt's pancakes and disliked how easily Jessica fit into the warm family scene, taking immediately to Leigh, Jarek's wife, now expecting their second baby and evidently blooming with happiness. Ellie, Mikhail's wife, who was in her last month of pregnancy, leaned close to her husband. Tanya, her child and Mikhail's adopted five-year-old daughter, was at preschool. Jarek and Mikhail's mother, Mary Jo, a long-legged Texan beauty, moved easily around her large, family-style kitchen with its strings of chili peppers, pottery and the sturdy Stepanov furniture. She was evidently pleased with her family and the presence of Jessica.

At the end of the table Fadey, Alexi's uncle, was obviously

enjoying his grandfather role. He cuddled and teased Katerina, Jarek and Leigh's toddler.

"We have traditional tea in the afternoon, if you'd like to come. The tea is called *zavarka*," Mary Jo was saying. "Fadey loves to have a family tea, and we brew it as he likes, in a *samovar*. We're looking forward to having Viktor here with us and sharing tea. It's so nice of Alexi to remodel the house for Viktor. We're hoping Alexi will want to stay here, too. Danya has already said that he might come, too."

"Of course. We are family, are we not? My wife makes the cookies like in the old country, raspberry, of course. My brother, Viktor, Alexi's father—he likes them, too. Thanks to Alexi, my brother will be joining me in his retirement. Viktor took some convincing. Alexi is a good boy—he helps with furniture loading and still he works at making a good home for his father. You will come, Jessica, to our tea. It is good to have women in a house—isn't it, Alexi?"

Alexi forced a nod and narrowed his eyes at Jessica, who was obviously enjoying his discomfort. Her smirks were even more delightful and difficult to resist than that beautiful temper, which set off her emerald eyes and red hair.

Today, seated beside him, with her face cleaned of cosmetics and her hair in a gleaming ponytail that swayed as she walked—her hips also swayed, and in the light lounging pants, they had been soft and warm and—Alexi forced his mind away from what his body wanted.

Jessica Sterling was a chameleon, a spoiled rich widow, used to getting what she wanted. The clean, wholesome look would appeal to the Stepanovs, and so for the moment she had shed her business skin.

Now Jessica was showing him that she could move into his life and ruin his peace—if she wanted.

Jessica smiled blandly at him and punched his shoulder lightly, playfully, like a girl tormenting a boy. "Alexi is a good old boy, aren't you, bud?"

"I am not a flower. Do not call me bud," he answered sullenly before he could shield his dark mood.

He frowned at Jarek, who had just whooped, and at Mikhail, who was smothering a grin.

Even worse was the look of the women around the table— softly pleased, hopeful for another wedding, another Stepanov wife that he would not provide. If he ever feared anything, it was women plotting a wedding. He remembered in every detail the arguments, the emotions, the costs—that hunted feeling....

When he turned to Jessica again, she was devouring her food, but that sly glance at him was victorious.

Alexi put out his hand and turned her face fully toward him.

She smiled innocently, but her dark green eyes sparkled with pleasure.

Alexi noted the light gold circle around her iris. He noted the smoothness of her skin beneath his touch. He noted the quiver that caused the tendrils beside her cheek to sway.

He noted the buttery gloss of her lips, the tiny crumb at one corner, dark with maple syrup.

He leaned down and kissed that portion of her lip, allowing his tongue to flick the crumb into his mouth. He sat back to watch, fascinated as she quivered and lit, almost like a colorful jewel with sparkling, shifting facets, her cheeks flushing again, her eyes bright and startled.

Recovering from the surprise he'd just given himself, Alexi began to smile—the game was his, unbalancing Jessica. Then he glanced at the other women who seemed breathless and waiting. Their dreamy expressions, those wedding looks, sent fear shivering up his nape and his smile died. "A crumb. She had a crumb on her mouth," he explained unevenly.

For once Jessica didn't reply. She simply sat with her head lowered, the sunlight gleaming on her dark red hair.

When lively conversation turned to his father coming in the spring, the remodeling of the house, the small pasture that was needed and tiny barn for the animals, Jessica still hadn't spoken.

She looked vulnerable and Alexi had the uncomfortable feeling that the blame was his. He wanted to run his hand over her head to soothe her—but that wouldn't do.

Instead he sipped his coffee and sat, very aware of the

woman at his side. To his disgust, Alexi wanted badly to place
his arm around Jessica, drawing her close and safe.

"It is a lonely time for a man without a woman at his side,"
Fadey was saying. "I am sorry your dear mother is not at
Viktor's side when he retires here. My brother still grieves for
her deeply. But Louise will always be in his heart, I know
this."

"Lovely woman," Mary Jo said in her soft Texan drawl as
she passed and placed her hand on Alexi's shoulder, leaning
down to kiss his cheek. "I'll pack lunch for you, darlin'. Are
you enjoying your stay at the Amoteh, Jessica?"

Jessica nodded and smiled. "It's lovely. I'm afraid I badly
needed the rest."

"A woman should not be working so hard that she forgets
she is a woman," Fadey stated softly. "You come to have
zavarka with us. It is good for a family to have this warmth.
When my brother comes, he will be pleased that you know our
customs."

"She's not staying," Alexi stated abruptly. This woman and
he were at war and it sounded like his family was making
permanent plans—

He already wanted Jessica in his bed, his lips tasting her
skin, her body flowing beneath his—

But she wasn't safe. Not a rich, spoiled, manipulative woman
who knew how to play games and land on her feet. Not a
woman with multiple surprising facets of loyalty, vulnerability
and an almost naive innocence that she fought to hide beneath
that sleek, polished exterior. The latter were probably well-
honed for deception, he decided darkly.

Jessica turned to him slowly, her expression set. "I'm taking
time to deal with a situation, no matter how long it takes."

Alexi's eyes locked with hers. He had his own situation to
deal with—one of a spoiled woman demanding his services.
Perhaps she needed to know how demands felt. "I am out of
coffee. Get me some, please."

Jessica didn't move, her green eyes narrowing. Alexi could
almost hear her silent reply—*Get it yourself.*

Then she smiled brightly and pushed back from the table. "Sure, bud. I'll just do that."

Then in passing, she riffled his hair as if he were a child. Instinctively, Alexi tensed, then he caught her wrist and stared up at her.

Still holding her eyes, wide and stunned now, he lowered his head. The kiss he placed in her palm was a challenge, not affection, he told himself.

In her suite at the Amoteh Resort, Jessica rubbed her hands together. She'd tried unsuccessfully to wipe away the feel of Alexi's lips, the flick of his tongue in the center of her palm.

The man moved quickly, instinctive, following his emotions. She hadn't expected either his kiss on her lips—"a crumb," he'd explained unevenly—or that kiss in her palm. Her eyes narrowed with the next thought: Alexi could just be raising the stakes of the game, challenging her. Jessica shook her head. That wouldn't do. She'd fought to survive and win all of her life—Alexi Stepanov would lose.

She pushed up the sleeve of her green merino wool sweater to reveal the wristwatch Robert had given her, and the emeralds caught her eye. He'd loved her green eyes—a sweet memory swept through her of how he had loved her, gently, unwaveringly, reassuring her constantly as, inexperienced, she'd moved in to take over his corporate position in Sterling Stops.

Her mind swung to another man, bold and arrogant and disdaining and proud. An irritating man who had tormented her. Alexi wasn't the easygoing man that he appeared—there were all sorts of layers brooding deep inside him. And a startling hunger that could reach out to burn her. Sexuality wasn't a commodity that had suited Jessica, and Alexi had definitely triggered a response she didn't want. He was at Willow's now, prowling through the situation for which Jessica was certain he could manage very well.

"Always use the best man for the job. That's what my husband used to say." After returning to the Amoteh Resort from the Stepanovs, courtesy of Mikhail, Jessica had promptly stepped into the shower. She had carefully refitted herself into

the armor of cosmetics and dressed carefully in her slacks and
sweater. The suite provided a business area and she was soon
wrapped in work that wouldn't wait. Howard had filled the
message machine, grilling her about Alexi Stepanov and pro-
viding information she had already obtained— ''He's there preparing a retirement home for his father. Alexi Stepanov actually
has nothing of his own. He tried to start a ranch and had to
sell at a loss.''

Her queries showed that Alexi sold at a loss because he
didn't want to stay in Venus, Wyoming, or in the home his ex-
fiancée had designed. Howard had been certain to slide in the
next bit of information— ''He's after your money, Jessica. A
down-on-his-luck cowboy, living off his father and looking for
a meal ticket. My father would not like you taking up with
him.''

''You don't know what Robert would want, Howard,'' Jessica stated coolly as she deleted all the messages and sat at the
suite's desk. She closed her eyes and thought of her husband's
last words. *I want you to be happy, my dear. I blame myself
for not spending enough time with Howard when he needed it.
Promise me that you won't ignore happiness when it finds you?*

Jessica rubbed the palm Alexi had kissed against her thigh.
The stirring of her senses, his arousal against her, the frame of
his strong body around hers as they rode to the Stepanovs' this
morning, disturbed Jessica. *Alexi Stepanov was six-feet-three
inches of pure trouble, not happiness.*

She looked out of the windows and thought of the Hawaiian
chieftain who lay in his grave on Strawberry Hill, amid the low
clouds and mist. He'd hated dying away from his homeland
and had leveled a curse against the land he could not escape....

Alexi Stepanov was definitely Jessica's curse.

But he was also a man that her instincts told her she could
trust.

The bell over the door tinkled merrily as Alexi entered Willow's Soaps. He noted that there was no burglar alarm or video
camera. Aware of his size in the tiny, cluttered shop, Alexi
moved carefully through the displays, the brochures about busi-

nesses in Amoteh and the tables filled with soap still in their molds.

In the off-season, the shop was quiet and scented. Alexi passed a stack of addressed shipping boxes. He noted a bowl of polished worry stones, probably from Ed and Bliss, who had settled in Amoteh. The parents of Leigh, Jarek Stepanov's wife, were carefree souls fitting well into the Amoteh community. A variety of love beads seemed to shift and glitter as Alexi moved by them, reminding him of the gentle lecture Bliss had given him about listening to his inner self, to align his chakras and let his female side emerge. A neat stack of her tie-dyed T-shirts lay on the counter where Willow had evidently been wrapping bars of soap in waxed paper and raffia, carefully labeling them.

Willow suddenly popped up from beneath the counter, her masses of waving black hair bobbing as she stared at him. Her little glasses were perched at the end of her nose, and she was wearing a battered sweat suit. Her eyes were rounded and filled with fear—"Oh, I thought you might be someone else—"

Evidently flustered, she recovered quickly. "Hi, Alexi. I'm just wrapping soap. It's a great ginseng and lemongrass blend. Smell—"

She pushed a tiny bar at him and added quickly, "For a woman, not a man. I don't stock the shop fully this time of year, but still, I do pretty good at Christmas. And your cousin, Mikhail, is just super, ordering my strawberry soaps for the resort, and I love the strawberry logo, and he gave me a good supply of them to label the soaps. Are you here to pick them up? I'm sorry, I don't have them ready, but I can deliver them right away. I just have to put the labels on them. I'm glad the gift shop is letting me put my shop's information on them, and I might start a catalog for people who want to order later, and did you want to buy something?"

Willow seemed to be desperately trying to conceal her anxiety. Alexi dutifully smelled the soap and handed it back to her. At the dance she'd seemed relaxed and delightful; now she was obviously tense and distracted. "Is something wrong, Willow?"

She shook her head and that hair, parted in the middle, quivered softly around her head. "Nope," she seemed to squeak in a high-pitched voice. "Just busy. I'm working on genealogy, you know, just getting the families of Amoteh, and I worked late last night. I have an apartment in the back and I heard a noise, and I—oh, it was nothing of course, but still I had a difficult time going back to sleep. It really was nothing, Alexi."

Too earnest in her denial, Willow was evidently hiding something. "The dance at the resort last week was really nice," she said quickly. "Thanks for dancing with me. I'm pretty clumsy. Um…did you come here for a special reason? I don't want to take up your time by chattering on and on, and I do that, chatter on and on—and I know you're busy working at the old Matthews place, fixing it up. And you bartend in your spare time, filling in. That's sweet of you. Oh, I'm supposed to go get Mrs. Black and take her to the beauty shop, and I— something came up and I forgot. I'd better call. Look around."

She hurried through the curtains behind the counter and Alexi heard her punching telephone buttons. "Mrs. Black, I'm sorry I'm late, but something happened last night—yes, I live alone, too, and I thought I heard someone at the door. No, I didn't call the police. It's just been weird here lately. I'll be right over. I just have to close the shop."

Alexi looked down at the computer-printed note on the counter: "W. You have made me angry. You will pay."

Jessica had been right; someone was bothering Willow, and she was obviously tense and upset. The telephone rang again and Willow answered cautiously, her voice hushed. "Please don't call again. Please," she pleaded.

Alexi picked up the bar of soap and compared the printing on the label to that of the warning note. It matched, but it could have been another machine like Willow's. Or someone who had access to hers.

When Willow pushed through the curtains, she was obviously upset, tears in her eyes. The odd smell of onions wafted from her and she pushed a cell phone into her pocket.

"I'll take these," Alexi said, and placed one of Ed's worry stones on the counter with some scented soap wrapped in raffia. "Do you know Jessica Sterling very well?"

Willow seemed nervous as she rang up his purchase. Then she looked over her glasses to Alexi and said very firmly, "She's my dearest friend. I think the world of her, and she's terrific. She's very special. Her beauty isn't only on the outside. I can't tell you the amount of times she's stepped in to help me, financially and emotionally. She needed a rest badly and I recommended the Amoteh Resort."

The onion scent was strong near Willow, but Alexi followed the obvious hint she had delivered. "You've been crying, Willow. Is there something I can do to help?"

He'd given her the opportunity to explain the onion scent, that she'd been cooking and that the smell had made her cry. Instead Willow glanced fearfully back at the curtains concealing the back room. "No...I...There's nothing wrong."

She turned and with a frown stared at the young man peering into her shop window. She made a hand-swishing "shoo, get away" motion at him. "That's Kapolo Jones. He's Ryan's friend—Ryan, Jarek's brother-in-law. Kapolo and Ryan surfed together and Kapolo just came up from Australia. He's told everyone he's a direct descendant of Chief Kamakani. He isn't. Kamakani was devoted to his one wife and Makamae died childless. That is well-documented, and he's angry with me for disproving his claim. It's like Elizabeth Price at the library telling everyone she's a direct descendant of—never mind, but that can't be true, either. I've got to go. Mrs. Black wants the discount the beauty shop offers today for tinting all-gray hair. Apparently blue is better. Do you mind?"

By two o'clock, Alexi had visited the library. The mention of Willow's name had struck fire in the librarian's eyes. She slammed down the Date Due stamp into the book of a waiting child. "I don't who she thinks she is, but that Willow person is dead wrong. I know my family tree."

Clearly, Willow had antagonized at least two locals—but she wasn't afraid of them. Her tears were probably due to the strong onion scent, and Alexi had begun to doubt danger to her.

Not ready to go back to his house, Alexi fought the memory of Jessica in his bed. He walked along the beach, inhaling the ocean-scented air. In the distance, a warning buoy rode the dark waves, clanging softly.

Alexi promised that he would forget her expression as he'd kissed her hand, how her eyes had rounded, and the scent of her had filled his senses.

He looked out at the huge waves, the layer of clouds obscuring the horizon. Jessica Sterling was exactly the kind of woman who could tear him apart—and Alexi didn't need a second go-round in that painful arena. He pushed back his hair and shook his head. But Jessica was nothing like Heather, not beneath the surface. There was too much heat, too much caring, too much sensuality. Or was that just one more deceitful example of how a woman could twist a man's insides?

And he knew he couldn't leave her alone. Not until he'd reached all the depths of her, explored them....

Alexi sat on a driftwood log, watched the seagulls forage amid the strands of seaweed and tiny shells. He poured the coffee from the thermos that Mary Jo had sent. He lifted his face to the wind and thought about the ancient Hawaiian's curse upon Amoteh, damning it for eternity because he'd been shipwrecked and stranded in a land that wasn't his.

Maybe the chieftain was lucky to live without the nettling presence of women, Alexi thought darkly.

And if Alexi had a curse, it was Jessica Sterling—as she had been this morning, sweet, vulnerable, a kitten at play. Alexi had seen his ex-fiancée at the same game—but with Heather, it was usually followed by a costly demand.

Jessica Sterling wanted something, too, but not for herself. She was all woman, soft and fragrant, and she knew how to bite back, how to defend herself, just the kind of woman who could tear a man's pride into shreds.

"Alexi?" Willow's soft voice interrupted his dark thoughts. "Mind if I share your log? You look so lonesome sitting here. The ocean makes this a peaceful spot, doesn't it?"

Alexi nodded, but he doubted that with Jessica around that he would be having "peace" anytime soon. Jessica had stirred his deep need for sex, and he wasn't a casual man, accepting one-night affairs to feed that elemental passion.

Moisture had steamed Willow's glasses and made her hair stand out in a huge ball around her head. "Do you like it here? I do. You seem to like the ocean. I'm surprised, really. I'd think you'd miss the mountains. I really didn't expect you to stay too long. The Stepanovs could have repaired that old house for your father."

"I like the mountains. I was raised in Wyoming. But I like it here, too."

"Good. I can't wait to meet your father. It's great that you're remodeling his place, though...I'm worried about Jessica. She seems upset about something today, all off-center, and that's not like her at all."

Alexi turned to the slight noise of someone walking over the wet sand. Jessica was marching toward them, her expression disdainful as she picked her way over the clumps of seaweed. One strand caught her shoe and she paused, lifting her foot to pick it away. She released the seaweed to the sand with a look of distaste and impatiently brushed her hands.

A rich woman, Jessica was out to make trouble for him, determined to get her way, no matter what the cost.

"Oh, hi, Jessica. Sit down with us." Willow looked up at Jessica, who was now scowling at Alexi.

"Are you sure I won't be interrupting?" Jessica said tightly as Alexi blandly met her furious stare.

In an upscale fleece jacket with a hood and designer jeans, she had replaced her cosmetics and her steely veneer. Her eyes blazed at him, her mouth tight within its gloss. Those silky waves weren't framing her face, an indication that she'd drawn it back into that sleek knot.

The sensual image of releasing that coil of hair into his hands stirred Alexi—just as he wanted to undo the woman, strip away all civilization between them, leaving nothing but heat and passion and pleasure.

Every instinct within Alexi told him that this woman could rouse and fascinate him like no other....

On the other hand, he'd already been torn apart by a woman just like this—one who knew how to get what she wanted....

Had Jessica used Howard, the man who had called her, and then moved on?

And had that affair been worth it to the man involved, the pleasure of having this woman?

Alexi lifted his face to the cold mist, inhaling it. She wanted something from him—to protect Willow, her friend. But what would Jessica want to sacrifice, to pay, other than money?

Jessica sat down beside Alexi, her anger simmering. She'd told him to stay away from Willow, who was sweet and innocent and not up to Alexi's overpowering male appeal. Jessica didn't seem to know that "potent" was a compliment to a man and her blushes had surprised him. For a sophisticated woman Jessica had surprisingly innocent edges to her.

Had his relationship to Heather been romantic? Or was it the satisfaction of needs—sexual and his biological needs for a home and children? And just maybe, the answer came back, Alexi did not want to know why he had planned a life with Heather. He'd known the reality of her coldness and yet— Was he so arrogant that he had thought he could make a loveless relationship become more?

Alexi looked down at Jessica's running shoes, now covered with wet sand. "If you stay here very long, you might think about getting a suitable pair of shoes," he said, reminding her of the expensive pair that had been ruined while hunting him last night.

Willow leaned in front of him to study Jessica on the other side. "Honey, you look absolutely drained. More business problems?"

"Not a problem in the world. I've just been sleeping and relaxing too much. I need something to do." Jessica hadn't been able to rest and she'd finally set out to run off her tension caused by Alexi's body holding her close on the ride to the Stepanovs' and that burning, unforgettable kiss in her hand.

Jessica noted how close Willow leaned against Alexi, trusting him. That wouldn't do. Willow formed deep attachments instantly and she was vulnerable and sweet. Alexi wasn't. Jessica had seen his true, dark, brooding, tormenting, irritating personality. And he was obviously sexually hungry—his arousal was hard to miss.

His blue eyes were searching her face now and deeper, to the things Jessica wanted to hide. He slid her jacket hood back from her head and studied her hair, brushed into its neat chignon. "I like you better without all that paint."

"Do you?" Suddenly, Alexi and Jessica seemed alone, tension sparking between them. "I…"

His hand had framed her face while the other hand was carefully removing pins. He dismissed her hands on his wrists, those soft fingers trying to waylay him. Alexi eased her waves round her face and he smiled softly, intimately, and Jessica's heart flip-flopped slowly, heavily, in her chest. "Hi," he said quietly.

"Hi," she returned breathlessly.

She glanced at Willow, who was obviously interested in the quiet exchange and leaning close. Jessica recognized Willow's expression from the last time Willow was infatuated; it said she was falling in love. It said that Willow pictured herself as the heroine of the Western movies she watched, riding off into the sunset with the cowboy.

Wounded in love, Alexi might need Willow's sweet, tender care for a rebound, but eventually he'd hurt her and Jessica couldn't have that. Jessica did the only thing she could to temporarily save her friend from Alexi Stepanov. "Willow, I've just got to get some gifts in the mail. Your soaps would be perfect. Do you think you could open the shop now, please? Sorry, Alexi, but I really need Willow now. You don't mind, do you?"

She stood abruptly and nudged her shoe to Alexi's boot, a warning to him to play along. His expression didn't waver, his steady brilliant-blue eyes startling amid his tanned face.

Jessica didn't want anyone to see inside her past the protective barriers to the private guilt and hurting edges. Alexi was circling her now, searching in emotional fields she wanted to forget—

He stood slowly in front of her, forcing her to look up at him, to be aware of how feminine she was in contrast to his

size and force—the contrast of a man and a woman, the phys
ical differences....

His hand raised to frame her cheek, his thumb stroking he
skin. Jessica shivered, not from the chill but from that quie
steady search of her eyes, as if he were seeing deeply inside..

"It is cold, Willow. I'll talk with you later," Alexi sai
without removing his gaze from Jessica's, and then he walke
away.

"See you later, Alexi," Willow called cheerfully. "I ju:
love the Stepanov men, don't you, Jessica?"

Not that one, Jessica decided silently. She rubbed her chee
briskly, trying to erase how easily those fingers had held he
how gently they had removed her hairpins. *Alexi wasn't at a
what he seemed to other people.*

In the shop Jessica collected a few assorted soaps and pai
for them. "I'll call the addresses where you can send these. I
that okay?"

Willow carefully began to wrap the fragrant seashell-shape
soaps into tissue, then tied raffia around them. "Great. Thank
You've helped me so much. Goodness, I've gotten so man
orders from the people who know you. I've been pouring mold
ever since the holidays ended, and I've reordered some gre;
scents and colorings, more seashell molds, too—the small kin
like for guest soaps. I think they'll sell well, don't you?"

"Yes, I think so." Jessica studied Willow. She seemed flu:
tered and hurrying through her words, her hands fluttering ov
her work, dropping one soap to the floor, raffia tangling in h
fingers. "Willow, I want you to tell me what is troubling yo
I know something is."

"Boyfriend trouble. You don't know him," Willow a
swered briskly. "That old Kamakani curse, you know. Bo
that Alexi Stepanov is sure sexy. I think he likes me. He w;
in here, looking around the shop, and he seems really nic
He's lonesome, I can just tell. Maybe I'll ask him over son
night for a movie and dinner. Oh, I suppose you could com
too," Willow added as an apparent afterthought.

"Thanks." Jessica didn't like the way Willow looke
dreamy and already in love, when she spoke of Alexi. And sł

didn't like the way Willow ignored the ringing of the telephone. "Shouldn't you get that?"

"No," Willow answered in a high-pitched tone, her expression too innocent.

"Is someone threatening you, Willow? I want to know—" She frowned as she noted the paper sack that Willow had just knocked over—it contained new packages of door locks.

Before Alexi and Danya had removed Lars Anders, the man had threatened a few women, a bully picking on the defenseless. Willow was totally trusting and afraid, judging by her darting quick look at the front window, the way she jumped at the slightest noise, a shutter banging in the wind. Jessica followed Willow outside and helped her secure the shutter, closing it. On impulse, she hugged Willow close against her. "You're like the sister I never had. I don't want anything happening to you."

Willow was suddenly calm, leaning back to smooth Jessica's hair. "I love you, too. Everything is going to be just fine. I knew it today. Everything came very clearly to me. I don't want you to worry anymore. It's time to love again."

Willow's statement would trouble Jessica for hours—until she decided to jerk Alexi, alias the "Sex Magnet," away from any Willow temptation.

Four

After a sponge bath, Alexi threw down the towel he'd used to dry his body and drew on his jeans. He stepped into comfortable worn loafers and shook his head as he traced the beam of light moving unsteadily from the resort toward his house. He quickly eliminated Marcella, who detested exercise; she wouldn't walk at night. At nine o'clock, that person was probably Jessica Sterling, the woman he most wanted to avoid—or to take into his arms, to taste that lush mouth—

Jessica Sterling stirred his senses, not a calm desire, either, rather a stormy passion he'd never revealed to another woman. His need for her was too immediate, too hungry, too elemental, just heat and storm—and for that reason, he'd stayed away from the Amoteh Resort. With Jessica under the same roof, sleeping in a bed nearby, he'd be—

Aching all over again, he reminded himself sharply—torn into shreds by a manipulating woman set on what she wanted and treading over anything and anyone to get it.

He should have known that a woman like Jessica, used to

getting what she wanted, would come after him—for his answer about Willow.

He looked at the sheets he had torn from his bed and stuffed into a pillowcase to be laundered. He had attempted to remove her scent—that erotic, feminine, sweet scent.

Didn't she know better than to come to a man's home at night? Wasn't she aware of what could happen—what was already happening between them?

Alexi pushed his hand through his hair and shoved the rush of questions aside. He moved to the outer door, opening it to better trace his invader. The path was dangerous and she could slip and—

Then he moved out into the night, whipped by wind and rain.

Cold weather always whipped his instincts, made them keener and lifted his need to hunt—

And perhaps to satisfy the sensual hunger that had been nudging him all day.

Intent upon the rocky, treacherous path before her, Jessica didn't see him standing silently as she passed. Dressed warmly in her hooded jacket, jeans and hiking boots, she looked small and vulnerable, like a woman who needed protection, who looked so lonely that she needed love.

"Jessica," he said quietly, and she stilled, the beam of light slashing into the night.

Alexi stepped behind her and when she turned, he caught her wrist, staying the flashlight from hitting his face. He didn't move, but a storm of images shot through his mind—that of Jessica prepared to defend herself—why? What had caused her to react so suddenly, as if she'd been attacked before and knew how to protect herself?

He could almost feel her heartbeat, the fear racing through her. Then the softening, the relief, the recognition in the wisp of her voice. "Alexi?"

Not "Stepanov" but Alexi. Is that how she thought of him? As Alexi?

"Yes, Alexi," he whispered, and followed his instincts to

calm her fear by placing his face along hers, to let her feel and catch his scent.

She hesitated momentarily, then moved close, her coat cold against his bare chest. Jessica was breathing rapidly, a release from her previous fear. She placed her forehead on his shoulder and her free hand opened on his belly, the glove warm on his skin. "You're cold."

"Yes. You should not be out tonight."

She lifted her face, scanning his. Inside the hood, drawn tight around her face, raindrops shimmered like silver on her skin. "I came for an answer. I couldn't find you earlier."

He'd gone to Kamakani's grave on Strawberry Hill, no easy path, slippery with ice and mud and snow. But once there, Alexi had removed his coat and had taken off his sweatshirt. He'd let the winds hurling up the cliff from the black ocean tear at him, an attempt to cleanse his need for this woman, who stirred him so primitively that he could barely keep his hands from her.

Now the wind hurled a slash of rain against him and Alexi moved to block the force from Jessica.

"You've been brooding again. You're so unpredictable and moody," she said quietly, and placed her glove against his cheek, rubbing it gently.

That unexpected touch soothed, and Alexi eased his face away. He couldn't have her reach into his heart so easily. "Yes."

"And afraid of me."

Alexi saw no reason to lie. "Maybe."

She slowly unzipped her coat and held it open for him. "You did this for me."

"There is a size difference," he reminded her, but stood closer and placed his arms around her. The coat barely fitted to his sides, but Jessica's arms circled him.

"I'm sorry she hurt you, Alexi."

"Maybe only my pride, not my heart. Which way are we going, you and I? Back to the resort? Or to my home?" Was he so hopelessly drawn to her, so needy of feminine comfort, that he accepted her so easily?

"I think we could speak more privately in your home," Jessica said quietly.

He turned and circled her with his arm, guiding her on the path toward the house. "Because?"

Resisting and wary, she moved slightly away, and instinctively Alexi tugged her back to his side.

"Because I'd rather discuss business privately. You have a way—like today at the Stepanovs'—of irritating me, of setting me off. That was unfortunate. I don't want another display."

"But you react so beautifully. I see more of you each time that surface is scratched, and I can't resist."

"I worked hard to get that 'skin.'"

Alexi didn't want to explore the hows with Jessica. She'd married a wealthy older man and ran a corporation—yet that image didn't match what he felt ran inside the woman.

What had happened to her? What was she hiding?

Inside Alexi's warm living area, Jessica removed her coat and tried not to look at Alexi's back as he bent to stoke the fire. Gleaming with rain and tanned by sun, his bare skin slid over powerful muscles. Her fingers ached to rub those shoulders, to soothe him as she had on the path. Alexi raised her feminine instincts and she wasn't certain that was good.

"About Willow. I've decided to call off the offer," she said suddenly. She feared the intimacy circling the room now, here with a man she barely knew yet trusted to protect her friend.

Why did she react to him so instinctively? How could she trust Alexi so quickly? After all the years of her struggle to be strong and independent, planning each move, scheduling her days, how could she trust a man she'd known only one week?

Alexi rose slowly and eased into the wooden armchair facing the fire. He leaned his head back against the cushion and closed his eyes. For the first time Jessica noted the cellular phone lying on the table, the laptop computer near it. A notebook was opened, a pen upon it, a calculator at its side. She hadn't thought of Alexi as a today-man, rather one who disdained technology and preferred his senses and the elements. She could have called him—but then, she'd really needed to see him, hadn't she? Why?

Jessica folded her arms around herself and stood in the shadows, studying Alexi's hard profile, the way his skin gleamed, defining his slashing cheekbone, the dark stubble of his jaw, that powerful throat, the muscles running into his shoulders.

"Tell me how you and Willow met." Alexi's deep, quiet command rocked the silence.

"Is it important? We're friends. I want her protected...but not by you. I'll find someone else."

"I want to know."

"All right—if you must. It was a simple meeting. Two years ago we were just two women who had entered a trade show bathroom. We shared a mirror and washed our hands. She used one of her soaps and I loved the scents and asked her about marketing them in Sterling Stops. A very simple meeting."

"Nothing about you is simple."

Willow had held Jessica as she'd cried—just simply opened her arms to hold Jessica, a new widow wrapped in grief and stunned at the heavy responsibilities ahead of her. She'd feared failure, and Willow had given her confidence during that dreary, fearful time. "She was there when I needed her most. I had just lost my husband. Willow is very dear to me. When the signs of danger to her started just before Christmas, I wanted to stay with her, but she...she wanted to keep me away. Probably to protect me."

"She's upset someone," Alexi stated quietly. "Or so it seems."

"You know that? What do you know?" Jessica came to stand beside him, fearing what he had discovered. "Tell me. It's important that I know exactly where you're at with this— she's so dear to me. You want the job because you like her— how much? How much do you like her?"

Alexi turned slowly to look up at her. "What is it to you?"

"That won't do, Alexi. Don't even think about it."

"I could move in close that way, to protect her and find out what she's hiding. I like her, too. What makes you think that I am unsuitable for her?"

He rose slowly to his feet to face Jessica. "This?" he asked rawly as he tugged her into his arms.

Jessica braced herself as his lips lowered, hovered over hers, and then Alexi freed her, stepping back to scowl at her.

She'd wanted him to kiss her. She'd wanted to taste him, to step inside those dark storms with him, to soothe him, to lie with him, skin against skin, hunger burning—

"It wouldn't stop at a kiss," he said unevenly, and pushed a hand through his hair. "And you know it."

"I want to go—" Jessica shivered, her body hungry for his touch, that near kiss lingering, nudging her….

Alexi's eyes glittered in the lamplight as his hand rose to curve around her throat, his thumb stroking her skin. "There's always a price, Jessica. You know it, and so do I. Here's mine—I want you to live with me, help me rebuild this place. It will appear as though we are lovers. The three of us will be good friends, and Willow will more readily trust me. I can watch over her…and you."

Stunned, Jessica shook her head. "I can't possibly live with you. I'm not the one who needs protection."

"I think you do. Mikhail tells me that a man is calling you, an insistent man, one who likes to threaten the staff. Frustrated bullies usually don't stop at threats."

Jessica rubbed her cold hands together. Howard's influx of calls had tripled today, his e-mail and faxes insistent—because of Alexi. Her husband had loved Howard dearly, and Jessica hadn't been able to tell Robert, a dying man, that his son was pursuing her. For seven years, before her marriage and after, Jessica had maintained a steady and businesslike distance from Howard, but the introduction of Alexi had set off his jealousy. "I can handle him."

Alexi's head inclined to her. "But I prefer to help you. That is my price to protect Willow."

"Forget about me. You know that she's in danger, then. Something *is* wrong. What?"

Alexi seemed to draw inside himself. "She isn't giving that away. But the signs are there. She's upset someone."

"That's exactly what I thought. She didn't come out and tell me exactly, but she's nervous when the phone rings. A window has been broken at her shop, and I found a note that she had dropped. It said that she was going to pay. She won't answer my questions—''

Jessica shook her head. ''I can't live with you. That's impossible. I run a corporation. There are basic daily duties. I'm quite safe, really.''

When had anyone but Willow or Robert been concerned about her safety? Jessica wondered. How could a man she barely knew want to protect her? Why?

Alexi shrugged, his expression unreadable. ''Your call.''

''You think I'll back off, don't you?''

''Maybe. Okay, I do. You don't really have to help me, but I'd like you to stay just the same. I can't really see you working with me, sawdust sticking to your sweat—oh, ladies don't sweat, do they? I can't see Mrs. Jessica Sterling hauling nails and boards around, breaking her fingernails.''

His face was in shadow and Jessica moved closer. Alexi knew how to push and so did she. ''You need me to pay for what she did to you, is that it?''

Those silvery eyes lowered down her body then up to lock with her eyes. ''You are a different woman.''

''How do you know so much? I married a much older man, didn't I? I'm rich and spoiled, right?''

''I think you loved your second husband very much,'' Alexi stated slowly. ''But you need me now, like it or not, and I'm involved, like it or not—with you. You want something from me. I want you to stay here, with me, where you'll be safe. That is my price.''

''I think you are living in the wrong century, Alexi. I can buy what I want.''

''Not me.'' He turned away and looked out at the night, his image reflected in the glass with Jessica's appearing to one side, her face pale, her fists clenched at her sides. Then he added a neat alternative, one he knew she wouldn't buy. ''Or I can start dating Willow. That would get me very close to the problem. If she doesn't want to tell a girlfriend, she might want to share with a man who is very close to her.''

"A lover, you mean?" Her voice was low and trembling with rage. "I told you, hands off."

Alexi turned to Jessica. What did he feel for her, this tenderness despite the fascination, the raw need of her? "You started this. Now finish it."

"You're not talking about Willow now, are you?" Jessica stared at the man challenging her. There was nothing sweet or gentle about Alexi Stepanov, the sensual sparks heating, sizzling, in the air between them.

She couldn't move as Alexi stepped toward her and took her face in his hands; his eyes slowly closed and his lips brushed hers. His kiss hovered and warmed and enticed, touching lightly at the corners of her lips, only to lift again and smooth her bottom lip. His smile curved against her cheek. "You're very warm, Mrs. Sterling."

"It's the wood stove."

"Uh-huh. And you're shaking. You want to run and hide, don't you? From me? From yourself? That's why you didn't go to the Stepanovs' family tea this afternoon, because you wanted to hide from whatever they are that frightens you."

Because she'd never been touched like this, she'd never had a man look so deeply into her eyes as if he found more than she was—more than she could ever be. And she had to know—what she could be, other than the woman who had survived and who never wanted to see her parents again. "This isn't about Willow at all, is it?" she repeated.

"No. But I will see to her safety. It would be easier to move closer to her, if you trusted me to be your friend, too."

"Your lover," she corrected.

"I would like that—yes, to feel your skin against my own, to feel you sigh as we make love, to taste your body, to feel your hands on mine. To see where this goes—or where it ends. But the choice is yours."

His honesty shocked Jessica as did the gentle way he drew her against his body, holding her easily. Alexi's uneven breathing and tense body said he was holding himself in check; Jessica sensed that he was letting her know and trust him. "I am very tired,'' she said, meaning it, as she leaned her forehead against his shoulder.

"You've come a long way."

"You don't know how far and how hard."

"Tell me."

Behind Jessica's closed lids, images of her girlhood slid by, the destitute living conditions, her alcoholic father and a mother who couldn't cope with a girl who wanted ''more'' and ''better'' and ''clean.''

And Jessica had married too young that first time, in her late teens, filled with hope—or was it escape?

Then Robert had desperately needed her to be strong, and somewhere deep inside was the girl that Alexi sought—filled with dreams and hope and laughter. That girl was safer, shielded and tucked away from harm.

The tear that had just slid down her cheek had slipped onto Alexi's broad chest, a silver trail on his tanned skin. Jessica realized that he'd taken down her hair, his fingers rubbing her scalp as he rocked her against his body.

She steeled herself against needing anyone, and pushed back from Alexi; she turned quickly before he could see into her unsteady emotions. "This is outrageous on both counts. I could make your life living hell—if I moved in here to play your lover.''

"You could," Alexi agreed easily.

"I'm going back to the resort."

"Ah, yes. Of course. To your safety, where no one can touch you…where you can issue your orders and yet retain distance from the world, from reality, from yourself. I'll walk you back, and don't argue."

"You'll see about Willow?"

She turned to see Alexi staring out at the night, his hands slid into his back pockets. He didn't seem to be a man who would turn away from a woman in danger. "You're going to take care of her anyway, aren't you? No matter what happens between us."

"Of course. I want you with me. It's that simple, and it's your choice."

* * *

In the furniture shop the Stepanov men sat around a huge, custom-made walnut dining room table, a canvas tarp protecting the glossy finish. A large plastic container of Mary Jo's raspberry-filled cookies sat on Fadey's stomach, his arm protectively around it as he munched on one. "So Jessica has gone back to Seattle. By the time she comes back, we can have it finished. Two days. No more. A bathroom for a woman. Alexi has already placed his order for new fixtures, and it will be delivered this morning. We can do that, eh, Mikhail? Jarek? What are men for, if not to make a woman comfortable where she stays, eh? We take out the old fixtures, put down new floor, a pretty little sink and mirror, a nice tub with feet."

"I don't know that she's coming back," Alexi stated carefully.

"Phooey. She will. You are a Stepanov man, are you not? She will come," Fadey said. He tossed a cookie to Jarek and another to Mikhail and then to Alexi. "This Jessica. I like her. And no, you boys cannot have all the cookies."

Fadey grinned widely. "I tell you what…we put in a good cooking stove, then Jessica can bake cookies—no more taking mine home with you."

"With a crew, we could put that house together in no time," Jarek offered.

"But then, Alexi couldn't get what he wanted, could he?" Mikhail asked smoothly.

Alexi shrugged casually, aware of how his cousins could tease him mercilessly. "She doesn't ask me to protect herself, only her friend."

Fadey tossed a cookie to the young man who had just entered the shop. Ryan Van Dolph, Jarek's brother-in-law, had the look of a surfer disgusted with winter weather. He caught the cookie, took off his coat and sat glumly, munching on the cookie. "What's up, man?"

"Alexi has a girlfriend. He needs the place fixed up fast so she can move in with him." Jarek grinned and placed a small bottle of orange juice in front of Ryan.

"Jessica hasn't made up her mind yet," Alexi returned. "So

if you're planning on teasing me about her, you could be wasting the effort.''

''Jessica Sterling is a powerful, hard-driving woman, who runs a big corporation,'' Mikhail said quietly. ''When she's at the resort, she puts in hard hours in her suite's minioffice. I can't see her stopping that. I wondered why she was here—a person like that is usually tied to her desk and not staying too long at a resort. Willow is her friend, but—''

''Someone is bothering Willow, and Jessica wants Alexi to find out who it is and stop it. That's why Jessica might live with Alexi—to stay close to her friend. It's not as if she couldn't just stay at the resort, or at Willow's, but oh, no. Our cousin here wants her to stay with him,'' Jarek briefly explained. He winked at Ryan. ''He's making his move.''

''Lay off,'' Alexi ordered firmly, and Jarek hooted, teasing his cousin.

Ryan shook his head. ''Kapolo hates Willow. He's supposed to be a direct descendant of Kamakani, and Willow has proof that he isn't. He's not the only one she's upset. She's been digging around family histories for a book on Amoteh and got a few people stirred up. She should just stick with her soap business. Hey, look at my folks, Bliss and Ed. They care less about a family tree, unless it's to hang tie-dyed T-shirts on or love beads.''

He sighed wistfully and leaned back to stroke the new surfboard leaning against the wall with a lover's touch. ''Man, I can't wait to start showing these babies off, Fadey. You think they'll really sell?''

''You and I are partners. Have I not said they would? You take these boards to Australia and Hawaii, swim with them and bring back orders.''

Ryan snorted and shook his head, covered with unruly blond curls. ''Swim? Man, I'm a surfer. I hit the big ones, go for the tunnel—''

Fadey nodded. ''Still. This morning we go to Alexi's and start making a bathroom for a lady.''

Ryan's disgusted expression turned into a big smirk. ''So finally, after everyone worrying about him, thinking of who they can set him up with, Alexi's got a girl. That ought to stop all the chatter between our women about finding him someone. Bliss is all worked up. She's been powwowing with Mary Jo, and Precious Child—my sis—and Ellie. If he hadn't come up with one soon, they were going to start importing a selection. He just saved himself a whole lot of trouble. Hey, maybe they'd do that for me—the homegrown chicks around here aren't digging me and it's a long time before the summer brings relief.''

Fadey tossed him another cookie. "Eat, boy. Then we'll go to Alexi's. It is time to make a bathroom for his woman.''

Alexi looked at Jarek and Mikhail and Ryan, who were all grinning at him. "Uncle Fadey, it's only a—it's to protect her.''

Fadey lowered his brows and frowned at Alexi. "Nephew. You want her. You want her with you. This is not so hard for a man to admit today, is it? That the man wants the woman? What is this modern thinking? She wants you—I saw it yesterday at breakfast. You talk to my sons, Alexi. They know how to get woman. Talk to your aunt. She came from Texas and her family didn't want this poor immigrant boy to marry her, take her away, but she come, anyway. Your aunt, she give me two fine boys with her green eyes. What is this wondering, this waiting—yes, okay, no, he wants her, she wants him? What is the problem here, nephew?''

"It's not that simple.''

Fadey threw up his hands. "Phooey. I say phooey. You are worried because she is a big shot. But yesterday, I saw a girl at my table. I give her big hug. There is no problem. You live together. You get to know the girl, she knows you. I have already called Viktor. My brother is happy for you. He has a troubling heart. You would trouble him more? Either this works or it doesn't. I can tell you, when your aunt and me—''

He looked around the table at Ryan and Alexi and his sons, who were all listening intently. Fadey cleared his throat and stated cautiously, "It is a good arrangement to get the girl to live with you, nephew. I say no more…. It's either that, or our women start this importing brides, maybe for you. Then, maybe they will have to stay at my house. I love women, of course, but I also do not like to wait for my bathroom in the morning.''

"I thought you weren't going to say any more, Pop," Jarek stated when he had finished laughing.

In the elegant Seattle home she had shared with Robert, Jessica slashed through paperwork that had been waiting for her signature. Unable to concentrate, she sat back in her desk chair, looked out into the late-morning drizzle and thought about Alexi.

In the middle of January, one long week had passed since Alexi had left her at her Amoteh suite door. He'd walked silently on the trail beside her, linking his hand with hers, offering a soft caution about a rock in the path. He'd waited as she placed her key card into the suite's door and opened it. "Don't be frightened, Jessica," he'd said behind her.

"I'm not."

"You are."

She'd turned slowly and looked up at him. "Alexi, I think you're on the rebound and hurting. Or you're out for revenge. Living with you isn't necessary. I don't understand you."

Those steady, silver-blue eyes hadn't flickered, denying nothing. "Your choice," he said quietly. "But I want you with me."

After a sleepless night, one in which she couldn't remove Alexi's light kiss at the door of her suite, Jessica had dressed quickly. She'd driven to Seattle and to safety—to what she understood and could manage. It wasn't possible to simply step into a life outside these elegant walls and the stress of a corporation—or was it? Was it only an enticing dream?

Jessica watched the ships passing by and thought of another waterfront, one with the Amoteh Resort overlooking it.

She mentally jerked herself back into her elegant Seattle office and tried to push away thoughts of Alexi. She tried to forget how her instincts had told her to wrap her arms around him, to kiss those hard lips and taste his hunger, meet it with her own.

Alexi stirred her sexually, that was all, she told herself, and sailed through another stack of paper. *A cowboy on the make and looking for a rich—* That image didn't fit Alexi.

Willow had wrapped herself into a tight wall of secrecy. Her replies to Jessica's queries gave nothing away. A window had been broken in her shop, but she was certain that it had only been a child tossing a rock—an accident.

Was it? Or was Willow in real danger?

"Thank you, Audrey." Jessica smiled briefly at her personal assistant who had just brought in a luncheon tray.

Audrey arranged Jessica's favorite dish, a Crab Louie salad, onto a table by a window overlooking Puget Sound.

Willow would be exactly what Alexi should have—a sweet, giving woman.

Alexi, on the other hand, wasn't sweet. Jessica had experienced the primitive male instincts that simmered beneath that rugged appearance. Whatever had run between Jessica and Alexi had been too instinctive to be false, too hot and hungry.

Maybe he just needed sexual relief. Maybe she did. Maybe it was just two people meeting at the wrong—or right time.... Maybe that's how one-night stands were done—needs met and fed, nothing more.... But with Alexi there would be more...and she hadn't allowed herself to be a woman for so long—if ever. Alexi made her feel—made her feel, senses hiked, anger, tenderness, fear, hunger.

Quiet and efficient, Audrey had gone back to her desk. Jessica stood and smoothed her hair in its neat chignon. She'd crawled out of a destitute situation, met Robert and had started a new life. Now he was gone and she carried on what he had loved, Sterling Stops. Jessica rubbed her emerald wedding bands; she wasn't a woman for a fling—or was she?

She'd heard about summer flings and shipboard romances from her friends.

Alexi wasn't a man to be forgotten—even now, she wondered how he would taste without that fine control, unleashing his hunger.... What instinct moved inside her to make that happen? Was it because she loved challenges, and Alexi was one big, fascinating temptation to step out of her box and live as a woman, to feel as a woman?

The brisk knock at her office door sounded before Howard pushed his way into the room. "So you're back."

He flung himself into a chair in front of her desk, jerked open his tie and stared at her. Howard looked like his father and, for a heartbeat, a sweet memory slid by Jessica. Then Howard's harsh voice cut through it. "So you've had a nice little holiday."

Jessica sat behind her desk, putting the distance and her official power between them. Perhaps Alexi was right about Howard—that he was furious another man had entered her life, that the ante had been upped. "It was nice—yes."

"I could have spent New Year's Eve with you."

"I assume you mean with your wife—together. I'm certain you could have booked into the Amoteh Resort if you wanted. The suites are beautiful, furnished with local artisans. The furniture is particularly unique, made by a local family, the Stepanovs."

Howard's expression tightened with anger. "You didn't return my calls and the resort's switchboard operator was uncooperative...so was the manager, Mikhail Stepanov. The Amoteh is one of the Mignon International chain, and I immediately called his boss. It seems as though Mikhail is well seated in the resort chain—he's married to the boss's daughter and apparently he is top dog there."

Jessica fought smiling, which would only antagonize Howard, and he was unpredictable when very angry. "What business did you have with me that was so important it couldn't wait for a few days? I never take a vacation and I needed a rest."

"You're a workhorse, Jessica. You never rest. I've seen you handle a twenty-hour workday and then take care of my father. What are you up to?"

She didn't want to tell him that Willow's calls had disturbed her and that she'd gone to help her friend. It wouldn't do to let Howard know that anyone was particularly close and dear to her. "What is the real problem, Howard?"

He lurched to his feet and walked toward the immense windows overlooking Puget Sound. He turned to her and his eyes glittered savagely, taking in her loose white silk blouse, neatly tucked into her practical but flowing black slacks. Aware of his unsteady nature, she never dressed casually when Howard might appear, needing all of her shields, her protections.

"Alexi Stepanov. You were with him, weren't you?" Howard accused.

"That's none of your business, Howard," she said, pushing down her anger. Howard had steadily inferred that she was his private property, just waiting for him to claim her, an inheritance of sorts from his father.

Howard shot facts at her like bullets. "You're a rich widow—my father's estate is in your hands and the majority of stock in a family-owned business. Fifty-one percent makes you quite appealing. Stepanov is a down-on-his-luck Wyoming cowboy. He started a ranch, built a house and had to sell. He's probably licking his wounds by taking the crumbs off the family table—he's a cousin of that Mikhail Stepanov."

Jessica did smile then. Alexi wasn't the begging sort. "You work fast, Howard. And you said all that before."

"He's out for your money. Don't have anything to do with him."

That curt order caused her to frown. If he chose, Howard could make life difficult for Alexi. "That's my business, Howard."

He slammed his fist down on her desk. "I'm making it mine."

In the next instant he had reached down and clamped his hands around her upper arms. He jerked her up against him.

"You're mine," he raged huskily against the cheek she turned to him, avoiding his kiss.

Jessica heard the door open—Audrey was always protective of her when Howard was near—

But Audrey stood at the side of a tall man with windswept brown hair and glittering ice-blue eyes. Alexi was wearing well-worn jeans and a denim jacket over a red-plaid flannel shirt—and an aura that bristled, narrowing the world to the drama between Howard and himself.

Her senses leaped, not with the fear of Howard but with a blast of pure happiness— She could almost feel herself in Alexi's arms, feel his heart beat against hers, as if he were the other part of her. She wanted to go to him, to have him hold her, to wrap her arms around his shoulders and tug his head down for a long, sweet kiss—and then she winced as Howard's fingers tightened on her arms.

"Don't look at him like that," Howard ordered roughly. "Look at me."

"Let her go—now," Alexi Stepanov ordered, his words quiet and dangerous. Without breaking his stare at Howard, Alexi sailed his tan Western hat onto a leather sofa. "Now."

"Get out," Howard growled.

Jessica understood the danger in the set of Alexi's body— that firm, dangerous stare. She eased away from Howard. "Howard, you'd better leave."

"Who is this jerk?" Howard demanded. "The handyman? You can wait for your orders in the kitchen."

Alexi's nod was almost polite. "My name is Alexi Stepanov, and now you will remove yourself...or I will do it for you."

"No one talks to me that way. *This is my father's house.*" But Howard was sizing up Alexi's stance and moving past him to the door. He paused and sneered at Jessica. "So this is your lover. Some cowboy who wants *my* father's money. You finally had an itch for a man, did you? So you bought this guy?"

Alexi tensed, but didn't move. His voice was deadly quiet, the accent clipping at his words. "Perhaps your father should have taught you manners. It is not too late for a lesson."

Jessica moved quickly to place her hand on Alexi's arm, to stay him from hurting Howard. His arm bunched beneath her touch and she could feel the anger vibrating off him. "I'll talk with you later, Howard."

But Howard had to have his last shot at her, words wrapped in a sneer that never failed to wound. "You know, Stepanov, she was just a clerk in one of my father's stores when they met. A poor little backwoods floozy with big hair and big ideas.

She got what she wanted—money, social position, this house. Maybe you two suit each other.''

The door slammed behind Howard, filling the room with ominous silence until Audrey opened it and quietly slid out of the room. Jessica walked to her desk and punched an intercom button. "See that Howard is out of the house, will you, Audrey? And lock the door behind him."

"He's gone upstairs to his father's old office. I think he's waiting for Mr. Stepanov to leave."

Jessica smiled briefly, coldly. In one way, Howard was totally predictable; he always met her low expectations. "I'll take care of him later."

"No, now," Alexi said darkly. "Which way is upstairs?"

Five

"It's not good to antagonize Howard. He can get nasty."

Jessica prepared to tell Alexi that she did not want him protecting her. The scene in her deceased husband's small upstairs office hadn't been pleasant. Howard had taken one look at Alexi looming behind her and had pushed out of the room with another parting shot. "I won't forget this."

Now Jessica turned from the dismal day outside her downstairs office window to Alexi, who was now seated on the leather sofa. His legs were extended, work boots propped over the daily newspaper on the coffee table. He looked tired, dark circles running beneath his eyes. He leaned back and closed his eyes.

Concerned for him, Jessica came to his side. "Are you all right?"

"I've been working hard and this last week the nights have been long. I keep expecting a woman with a flashlight to come walking from the Amoteh." His hand eased to smooth her thigh, pressing just enough on the loose slacks to find her body.

"How long have you been dealing with the way he treats you?"

Jessica moved back just that fraction, uneasy with Alexi's sensual, stirring touch. "Howard has never acted like that. It was worse today. What about Willow? Have you found out who is bothering her?"

Alexi's eyes slowly opened to look at her. He took in her smooth chignon, the careful makeup, her loose silk blouse neatly tucked into her flowing slacks and the black low-heeled pumps. "He wants you badly. He wants to own you, to possess you."

She shrugged lightly. "I know. He's not getting me. I'm just a challenge to him."

"You are definitely a challenge—mine." As if testing her, Alexi moved slightly, just enough to bring him closer; he continued to slowly stroke her thigh and up to her hip, following the curve with his open hand. She eased back once more, unsettled by how much that easy touch could make her ache for more.

Alexi smiled slowly, warmth smoothing away that hard, taut look. "It will be worse now. Now that he knows you have a…'lover.'"

She crossed her arms. "You just love to push, don't you? We both know that isn't true. I've been the object of gossip for years. I can hold my own."

"Of course. You're very independent. You're afraid you'll look weak if someone helps you, aren't you? You try harder because you're afraid that you might fail, and failure isn't allowed?"

His accurate perception startled her. She'd failed with her family and she'd failed with her first marriage, and she'd battled those insecurities all of her life.

With another quick insight into her life, Alexi pinned a deep-rooted problem that Jessica had expressed to no one. "It's important to make a child feel strong and secure, isn't it? To love them?"

"I don't know," she lied, flashing back to her childhood

where she had to scramble for attention. "I've never been a parent."

With a quick movement Alexi's hand tugged at the back of her knee and she toppled onto him. He caught her and turned her body to cradle her against him. His lips brushed the corner of hers and he whispered unevenly, "So, then, you are happy here? In this big house without me?"

"I have been. Alexi, let me up." But even as she spoke, her hand was running beneath the heavy flannel-lined denim jacket to the collar of his shirt, seeking entrance to that warm, smooth skin. She had missed him desperately in the past week, her nights as sleepless as his.

"I want to make love to you now, so you won't forget me," he said roughly, his head tilting just that bit to capture her hand against his throat.

"But you won't."

His whisper against her throat was low and sensual. "I haven't been invited properly. It is for you to choose."

The brisk knock on the door signaled Audrey's entrance with a serving tray. "I thought a man like you could use a meal. I whipped this up myself. I hope it is all right."

She beamed at Alexi who immediately lifted Jessica and plopped her down beside him on the couch.

Jessica smoothed her hair, shaken by the steamy sensuality that had just passed between them. A man who moved quickly, Alexi's expression had changed to that of a man eager for food. She inhaled slowly, nettled somehow by the distinct feeling that she was no longer the main course. But that was ridiculous, of course, her mind told her body. She met Alexi's quick study of her. "You know what you're doing every minute, don't you?" she asked unevenly.

"No," he returned too abruptly. "With you…no."

Alexi stood to take the large tray from Audrey. "This looks delicious. Thank you."

A middle-aged woman and happily married for thirty years, Audrey blushed. "My boys were always hungry, too. Mrs. Sterling's lunch is on the table. Make sure she eats something, will you? She's been too quiet. Something has been bothering her since she got back last week from her holiday. You're one of the Stepanovs who make that beautiful furniture, aren't you? And related to Mikhail Stepanov, who manages the resort where Mrs. Sterling stayed?''

Alexi acknowledged the relationship with a slow nod. "My cousin. There are lots of cousins in our family."

Before Audrey left the spacious, elegant office, her warm smile at Jessica said she had connected her employer's restlessness to Alexi. Jessica thought she heard Audrey whisper, "About time."

Alexi placed the tray on the coffee table and glanced at Jessica, who had settled back to frown at him. "You heard her—eat."

"Tell me about Willow."

Jessica watched Alexi place the tray on the table, remove his jacket and sit beside her. As if just remembering, he picked up his jacket and removed a small foil-wrapped package. "Raspberry cookies from my aunt."

From another pocket, he took a bar of Willow's ginseng and lemongrass soap. "I smell like a woman. I came to Seattle to collect special hardware for Fadey's chests and in the store, men smile at me like I am wearing perfume," he said, the words filled with male disdain.

But Jessica was holding his wrist and looking at the blisters running across his broad palm. "Give me your other hand."

She placed the soap aside and held his wrist as she took his other hand. The dark red angry spots on both hands caused her to ache. She searched his expression. "These must be painful. You're an experienced workman. What happened?"

"Are you coming back with me?" he said quietly, ignoring her question.

Are you coming back to me?

The question was so simple and yet layered with complexities. It caught her, holding her. She'd dreamed of Alexi every night and thinking of him had taken most of her days. It would be so easy to—

Jessica hurried to get the tiny first-aid kit from her desk drawer. Seated beside Alexi, she smoothed antibiotic cream over his hands and bandaged them in gauze. "It isn't that bad," he said, watching her. "I was only chopping a little wood."

"This looks like you chopped a whole woodpile in one try. Tell me about Willow."

"I was missing you." He hesitated and toyed with her ear, running a fingertip into that smooth chignon. He eased free a strand to wrap it around his finger, studying the shades. "I think there is a need of you in Amoteh—yes. Are you safe here, Jessica?"

"Yes. I've made it quite safe for myself."

"Your husband's office. You have kept it the way a man would like."

"Robert worked as long as he could. Sometimes I think that was what kept him going."

"You loved him." It was a statement, not a question, and Jessica slowly nodded.

She looked down at the big hand holding hers, fingers intertwined, dark against pale, male and female, the sharp contrast she always felt with Alexi. Whatever ran between them, it was more elemental than what civilization could conceal. Even now, her senses were leaping, heating, and Alexi was looking intently at her, as though he were catching those sensual waves and they churned his own.

"You're afraid. I understand. You've wrapped yourself in one world, and another would tear this one apart."

"I don't know what you're talking about." But she did and amended, "I've never been a gambler."

Are you coming back with me...to me? had sounded so simple, exploring herself as a woman, grasping with both hands what Alexi could give her—the feeling that she was a woman and not a machine.... The thought beckoned and enticed.

He turned from her to the meal Audrey had just prepared and delivered—a huge glass of milk, a big grilled steak with fried potatoes, a mound of green beans and two slices of buttered Texas toast. The slice of apple pie was actually two pieces that had been warmed, with a mound of ice cream over the top.

He dug into his meal, apparently forgetting Jessica and the

drama that had just passed. "I love that woman," Alexi stated almost worshipfully between bites.

Jessica carried her salad to her desk. She picked at her food and watched Alexi, who was clearly enjoying his meal. Once he had eaten, she'd…she'd invite him to stay. She'd invite him into her bed and rid herself of her need for him. Then it would all be over—that trembling hunger that had just spiked at the sight of Alexi.

While she was sorting through the right words for a proper proposal, Alexi wiped his lips with a napkin and stood. He drew on his jacket and walked to the desk. Jessica held her breath as he looked down at her.

Then he punched the intercom button that read Audrey. "Audrey, I love you. Come visit me at Amoteh. The meal was very good. Thank you. Where should I bring the tray?"

On the other end of the line, Audrey sounded as if she was beaming. "I'll take care of the tray. You just come back, Mr. Stepanov."

"You call me Alexi. Please take care of Mrs. Sterling."

Before Jessica could say anything, Alexi was striding toward the door and opening it. His expression had hardened, those blue eyes cutting at her from across the room. "Thank you for the hospitality and for pointing me to Willow. She's sweet. Without you, I might never have gotten to know how great she is."

Jessica stood abruptly. She knew how potent he could be, how tasty, how good Alexi felt to a woman's body— He would roll over Willow like a steamroller. Willow would be absolutely defenseless against his seduction…. "You leave her alone."

"Ah. You want me for yourself. Then you will have to come and get me." Alexi smiled briefly, wolfishly, then closed the door quietly behind him.

"He's got a high opinion of himself—" In spite of her caution to ignore his taunt, Jessica rounded her desk and flew across the plush office carpet. She jerked open the door and ran straight into Alexi, who had apparently been waiting for her.

She heard her own soft explosion of breath leaving her body as he tugged her hard against his body, his arms wrapping around her, his hands open, pulling her even closer—

She saw his primitive expression before his lips came down to fuse with hers. One hand cradled her head for his kiss, fingers delving deep into her hair, spearing through the pins anchoring it.

She caught his scent—the contrast of Willow's soap with the dark masculine layers beneath: a blend of smoke and freshly cut wood, and impatience, of sensual hunger. Her arms raised to claim him, her fingers locking on those powerful shoulders, because Alexi wasn't leaving her, not until she'd taken what she wanted—

With a rough sound of pleasure deep in his throat, Alexi lifted his head for just a heartbeat, his eyes glittering down at her. There was no tenderness in his expression, only the hard demand, and the question—would she answer his hunger?

Or would she deny her chance to feel like a woman, to hold and equal a man's passion, to experience what other women had known?

Then she was moving into the fire, opening her lips, slanting just that bit to allow for a better fit—her hips moved at the pressure of his open hand, pressing her against him as Alexi moved their bodies back into the office.

A hard nudge of his shoulder shoved the door closed and she heard the click of a lock being turned.

Breathing hard, straining for breath and fighting to step outside this moment to reclaim herself, Jessica saw her hand lift to Alexi's hard, warm face.

He turned to kiss her palm briefly. "This is what I know," he whispered unevenly before she raised on tiptoe to kiss him again, to open her fingers through that thick waving hair, to hold him still for what she wanted—for what had simmered in her for days—this taste, this man.

She fed upon those dark, brooding layers, the arrogance, the tenderness, the hunger that matched her own. She pressed her lips against his jaw, felt that snap within him, the lock of his biceps moved against the sides of her breasts, and then Alexi's big hands were smoothing her body, stroking her hips.

He pulled back and, holding her, looked down at their bodies, pressed close. He studied her face and then eased his hand over her breasts, caressing and cupping them slowly, gently.

Jessica wanted more. *More.*

She wanted his skin against hers, and her fingers trembled as she eased his jacket away.

Alexi held very still, watching her as she fumbled with the buttons on his shirt, opening it. His breath hissed by her cheek as she bent to nuzzle his bare chest, to kiss that smooth, hot surface, to rub her face against the wedge of hair, inhaling his scent, drawing it into her.

Between their bodies, Alexi's hands moved, opening the buttons to her silk blouse, tugging it away from her body. She stiffened, her head back, uncertain of herself, and yet the woman within her dared, challenged Alexi to take what he wanted—what she wanted.

Holding her eyes, Alexi unfastened her bra and, uncertain now, Jessica's hand pressed the lace close to conceal her body. He bent slowly and nuzzled her body, her breasts, as she had done for him, and his open lips moved across her skin, burning it, until they found that hard peak of her nipple.

Alexi's mouth was warm and gentle, and waves of heat pounded at Jessica, her body trembling as she watched his dark skin, his hair, move against her pale skin. She forced away her hand and dropped the protection of lace, allowing him more access, her body clenching with each tug of his lips, each gentle bite.

With a rough sound, Alexi tugged free the button of her slacks, impatient with a second button, tearing it away to find her zipper.

Slowly, so slowly, while his lips teased hers, he stroked the slacks from her hips. They fell to her feet and Jessica arched up against Alexi's body as she stepped free of her clothing.

There in the shadowy, elegant office, with the rain pattering softly at the window, Alexi looked down at her body, at the champagne lace on her boy-cut briefs. Shaking with need, fearing what ran deep and wild inside her, Jessica tried to cover her breasts with her arm, but Alexi eased it away. "I want to look at you," he whispered.

Then he added gently, "You're embarrassed."

"We're in my office and it's hardly the place—"

"That's not it. The windows have a privacy film and there is no one but you and I here…. Have you never had a man look at you?"

She shook her head, trembling now, uncertain of herself. She leaned her forehead against his chest, unable to meet his eyes, to explain. "No."

Alexi held her away from him and tilted her face up to his. "You have been married twice."

She tried to laugh but it came out unsteadily. "It's been a long time."

It had been forever….

"Tell me." Alexi eased her against him and Jessica wrapped her arms around his body, fearing to open herself to him, to reopen her past. He smoothed her hair, kissed her cheek and caressed her back.

"There's too much." Where could she start? As a hungry, untended child? As a teenager who thought marriage would take her away from her family? From her first husband, who roughly fumbled through their wedding night and bragged about it to his friends? Or to Robert, who had only touched her with tenderness and pride?

Her emotions churned within her, because this one man had touched her deep inside, to that delicate softness she'd protected for a lifetime. She wanted to feel everything all at once with Alexi—every hunger, every caress—to allow herself to open fully, to demand—

Alexi's chest moved slightly, side to side, pressing against her bare breasts. "I like this," he said quietly against her ear, "you resting against me, soft like this."

"Stay with me."

"No."

She opened her lips against his shoulder and felt the shudder of reaction go through his body. "I could make you."

"That remains to be seen—if you could make me."

Jessica didn't trust the humor in Alexi's tone and turned her face to his throat, nipping lightly. "You want me."

When he didn't answer, she drew back to study his expression.

He was grinning. "One of us still has most of their clothes on. That says something about who can make whom."

Jessica pushed back from Alexi and crossed her arms in front of her breasts, concealing them. Sensitized, her nipples peaked at the touch and she frowned up at Alexi, who was buttoning his shirt. "You're a difficult man, Stepanov."

"So you say."

"Tell me about Willow."

He put on his denim jacket and reached for his hat. "Find out for yourself."

"Damn you. You like pushing me, don't you? Does bringing me to heel, making me come to Amoteh, working on that house, have anything to do with making your ex-fiancée pay for what she did? Am I paying her tab? Is that what you want? Revenge on a woman who walked out on you?" Jessica demanded hotly. "Do you still love her?"

Alexi's blue gaze pinned her. "You're asking a lot of questions."

No one had ever gotten to her emotions as Alexi had, and Jessica struggled to squash her simmering temper. In another minute she'd drag him back to that couch and wipe another woman from his memory— That primitive instinct shocked her. She usually planned her life and Alexi was— "You've just walked through my life. I deserve to know about yours."

"Then you'll have to come after me. Let's have this out, shall we? Or are you too afraid to take a chance?"

At eight o'clock on the evening after Alexi had driven to Seattle, he couldn't concentrate on the figures for repairing his father's future home—or on building enough of a down payment on the Seagull's Perch.

He'd been unable to stay away from Jessica any longer, and the week separating them had seemed an eternity.

He needed to feel her against him...to see that pale skin against his own, the softness of her breasts against his chest, the taste of her, the sound of her breath—uneven, as if her need had trapped it within her—need for him....

The kiss was to reassure himself that Jessica hadn't forgotten what ran between them, not only the passion, but the tenderness, too.

The excuse to see her was just that; the cookies he'd taken her were his, baked by Mary Jo, the soap had been purchased especially for the woman he wanted.

Willow was clearly framing her own danger, magnifying it only to Jessica, who had been calling nightly—and once when Alexi had been in the shop. He'd listened intently to Willow's innuendos of danger from the back room; he'd followed her handwritten checklist tucked into a crime detective manual on dealing with stalkers. He'd compared her carefully placed, threatening notes to her computer printouts and linked the paper and fonts together—Willow was creating her own threats.

The window that had been broken recently had been hit from the inside of the building. The shoe prints in the flower bed beneath the window said that the prowler had small, narrow feet, not filling the overlarge boots.

Kapolo would wear a large-size boot—and so would the librarian, Elizabeth Price.

Alexi had seen Willow in action—emotionally defending her expertise and what she had uncovered about their faulty genealogy. She didn't fear either opponent.

In Alexi's appraisal of the situation, Willow clearly was framing her own danger and using it to worry Jessica. Willow's purpose? To draw Jessica back to Amoteh.

But why?

Before he had left to see Jessica, Alexi's quiet, intuitive question had stunned Willow. "Are you playing matchmaker, Willow? With Jessica and me?"

Willow's wide-eyed expression was too innocent. "Um. Maybe. But for a good reason. I can't bear for her to stay in that big empty house, that shrine to her dead husband with that worm Howard hovering around her."

"That description fits," Alexi had said very quietly.

"Then you'll play along? Let Jessica think that she needs to visit me more often?"

He'd smiled at that. "Maybe I'm the one she wants to see. It's her choice. I've offered her a job."

"Really? Doing what?"

"My assistant with no pay."

"Aha!" Willow had exclaimed. "The plot thickens. You want her. She's been independent for her whole life. She might not like a takeover. There's a lot going on inside Jessica that no one knows. I hope you know what you're doing. For both your sakes."

In his house, Alexi stared out at the rainy night and smoothed his lips with his fingertip. He still tasted Jessica, that quick fire between them, the urgent hunger that was too real to deny. Wounded once, a man's pride was important. He needed a sign that she matched his hunger, his needs, with her own. Jessica already knew he wanted her. *Would she come to him?*

He rubbed his chest, remembered the softness of her breasts against him, the satin of those lace briefs, the loose leg openings that could so easily be breached.

But the ache that rested within his heart needed more than a quick sexual fix. Alexi needed to care for Jessica, to protect her now, to enjoy the colors flashing beneath the cool, professional surface.

When questioned about her late husband, Jessica's expression had softened. She hadn't changed his upstairs room, or the sitting room next to it—where a man's big chair and reading lamp could be seen through the open door, a stack of magazines and books beside it. Men's bedroom slippers rested on a footstool.

Alexi remembered Howard's grasp of Jessica's arm. Howard's furious expression said he would rape a woman to prove that he was her master and a man, if that's what it could be called.

Alexi tried once more to make sense of his notes on the

Seagull's Perch, the repairs needed to it, the necessary budget-type remodeling.

But his mind came back to Jessica. In her office she'd collected her dignity, walking away from him to take a black kimono from a rack. With her back to him, she'd belted it, and the red silk dragon curling on the back looked no more primitive than his need to take her.

When she had turned, her auburn hair shining against the black satin of the jacket, she'd pulled herself back into her businesswoman shields.

Jessica knew how to survive, how to protect herself.

Maybe it was time someone else helped her.

Alexi stared grimly at his empty bed and the vision of Jessica, snuggled deep inside it, tormented him.

Maybe Kamakani's curse was true—that Alexi had lost his pride once and now his need of another woman could cause him to lose it again.

She would return to Amoteh for Willow.

But would Jessica come to him? Would she stay with him and not in an Amoteh Resort suite?

Alexi looked at his reflection in the glass window. A hard man stared back, his deeply set silvery eyes glittering, his expression a stern mask of jutting bones, more shadow than light.

Perhaps Kamakani's curse had struck him, a proud man wanting a woman to bend just that bit—to salve his pride.

He stared toward the bluff on Strawberry Hill, that peninsula spearing out into the black Pacific waves, now separated from land by high tide. Chief Kamakani had gifted him with the curse of a woman—Jessica.

Jessica pulled her BMW off to one side of the road above Amoteh. In mid-January, the rain beat steadily down on her car, the windshield wipers click-clacking. It had only been a little over two weeks since she'd danced with Alexi, and now her desire to see him wouldn't be ignored.

He'd just fired her need for him by appearing at her office that morning. Alexi knew exactly what he was doing.

Jessica gripped the steering wheel. She wasn't an impulsive

woman. In fact, she kept herself on a meticulous, planned, thoughtful life schedule. Now, here she was, determined to see Alexi. He was volatile, moody, brooding over a woman who had wounded him—and most likely wanting another to pay.

But Jessica knew that Alexi wasn't as Howard had labeled him: "a down-on-his-luck, out-of-work cowboy, living off his relatives, and tending bar and probably women for his meal ticket, if that's what it could be called."

After another episode in her running battle with Howard, Jessica needed Alexi's safety—and his hunger. "If his feelings for Heather have anything to do with this…"

With a last indrawn breath to brace herself, Jessica stared into the night toward Chief Kamakani's grave site. "You're pretty good at this cursing business, Chief. I was safe and knew exactly what I was doing. Now I don't. I've known Alexi for just over two weeks and here I am, delivering myself on a platter. I could walk away from this, but I'm not going to," she whispered, and then slid the car into gear.

Was Alexi's hunger, his kiss, everything that she remembered? Or was she just dreaming? Was she so wrong to want him this passionately? To feel the intensity of life that she'd never known with a man?

Alexi noted the headlights of a car spearing into his darkened room. He stood by the window as a sleek, upscale car pulled beside his work truck. Head bent, her coat gathered around her, a woman hurried toward his back porch.

Jessica! He walked to the living quarters door, opened it and a blast of cold air from the sunroom hit his bare torso.

He jerked open the exterior door and stared at the woman smiling up at him. "Hello, Marcella. Out late, aren't you?"

Alexi frowned at the second car that had pulled alongside the road, the headlights shooting off into the rain.

"I've come to play," Marcella whispered sexily, and lifted the resort's basket, used by guests for wine and dinners along the beach.

Her raincoat gaped open to reveal that her body was nude, except for thigh-high black panty hose. With an alluring look, she nudged past him. On high heels, she picked her way over the heavy utility electric cord and rough board floor to the door of his living quarters.

Alexi stepped outside, slammed the door behind Marcella and ran for the car parked on the road. Through the veil of rain, he'd seen Jessica's face, framed by the dashboard's light. He jerked open the passenger door and slid inside just as Jessica prepared to put the car in gear.

Alexi switched off the key and pulled it from the ignition. "This isn't what you think," he stated unevenly, because he read Jessica's wounded expression too easily. "I am not having an affair with her."

"You're in demand. I'll say that for you. Is Heather arriving, too?" Her words were cutting and cold, and she was shaking, her arms wrapped around herself.

Alexi picked up the cell phone she'd been using and dialed Mikhail's personal number. His cousin wouldn't be happy, but neither was he. "You have a guest who has strayed onto my premises—yes, Marcella. Come get her. I will be waiting in another car. Thank you."

Jessica stared out into the night as if she were disinterested, but Alexi noted the quick trembling of her lips. "I did not invite her," he said.

Her flat "Sure" was disbelieving.

"I don't lie. And when I say Heather never touched what is inside me, I mean it. It took an irritating, fascinating sexy redhead to do that." He noted the packed bags in the back seat. "You came to stay with me."

"No. With Willow. Or at the resort. Definitely not with you," she answered loftily.

"Liar." Alexi slid his hands beneath Jessica's body and lifted her from the driver's seat onto his lap. "I'm cold, you know."

Jessica sat very straight and looked out at the rain. "That is not my problem. I'm sorry that I irritate you, but the feeling is mutual. You like to make my life difficult. You revel in—"

"But you're so warm and soft and sweet." He couldn't resist

teasing Jessica as she sat so straight on his lap. Would she leave now?

"You're so full of it. You'd better get in there. Your girl-friend is waiting." She traced the sleek BMW that had just parked next to the other car. Mikhail Stepanov, looking very formidable, stepped out into the rain. He lifted a hand in Alexi's direction and then strode toward the house.

In two heartbeats Mikhail came out the door, hauling Marcella by the back of her coat collar. He ignored her swatting hands, ushered her into her car and stood as she rolled down the window to argue. Whatever passed between them wasn't pleasant. Marcella gunned the powerful engine, reversed and soared away toward the Amoteh Resort. Mikhail turned toward Jessica's car and, with a curt nod, slid into his own BMW and drove toward his home and family.

For just a moment Alexi almost felt sorry for Marcella. She appeared lonely, but driven. Marcella appeared to place value on how she could attract and have men, not in her esteem as a woman. In his arms was a real woman with heart and compassion and strength and intelligence.

And a body that was sheer temptation. His hand slid over Jessica's hips and accidentally inside her coat. His fingers locked onto smooth, bare, warm silky flesh and he forgot about everything but the woman in his arms. His voice seemed to echo rawly, unevenly, against the plush interior of the car. "Jessica. You are not wearing anything."

"Apparently it isn't a novel idea where you're concerned. I saw her getting out of the car. She must have been freezing. Gee, and me without a wine basket. You should have taken the first offer. The benefits were better."

But Alexi was carefully unbuttoning her raincoat, dismissing her attempts to close it. His hand skimmed her body from her thighs to her stomach and upward to cup her breast. "Are we headed for make-up sex?"

Jessica shook her head and stared down at him. "You could drive anyone over the edge and make them wonder what they're doing."

"I can only try, sweetheart," he said, and watched her eyes darken as his hand slid lower.

While he caressed her softness, Jessica held very still as if locked in pleasure, unable to move. "You'd better stop that, Alexi," she whispered breathlessly.

"Why?" But he was already bending to taste her body.... "Do you want me to?"

She could barely breathe, his lips trailing over her skin, nuzzling her breasts, his hand warming her thigh—"Don't... stop."

Six

The offshore buoy clanged softly in the night, the sound echoing in the salt-scented wind as Alexi carried Jessica toward his home. Unhurried, he walked as if the cold rain wasn't pelting his body.

The gesture appeared primitive and possessive. It called for a response to equal his elemental ones and Jessica gave way to the soft, feminine instincts to put her arms around him, to trust him. She eased away his hair from his cheek and wiped the raindrops from his eyebrows. The stroke of her fingertips smoothed the dampness from his sharp cheekbone.

Instantly, Alexi tensed as if caught, entranced by the unexpected; he paused and stared down at her. Her hand was still on his cheek and she lifted to kiss him lightly. For a moment his harsh expression eased and he took the second kiss, which came to her as a tender reassurance, a sharing of something deep inside him, a contrast to the primitive hardness just heartbeats ago. Her instincts moved her now and Jessica nestled her face against his throat.

Inside the living quarters, he kicked the door shut and stood holding her as if he didn't want to release her body. He sniffed lightly, impatiently nuzzled her face with his cold one and lowered her to her feet.

"That woman wears too much perfume." In the next heartbeat he was striding to the windows, opening them and the door to the deck.

He opened an interior door and peered inside. "Good. She hasn't been in the bathroom. It's for you. I'll get your things and move the car."

"There's no need—"

Alexi's expression was fierce. "You're staying. Her smell will be gone in a minute."

"You don't have to explain, Alexi."

"I did not encourage that woman. I have told her that I am taken. When I go to the Amoteh, she stalks me. I have taken refuge here, and yet still she comes," he stated with disgust as he bent to stoke the wood fire.

Then he stood to look at Jessica and his words were crisp with frustration and trimmed with his slight accent, the abrupt, old-fashioned phrasing. "You know that I am waiting for you. That this is right. That I have no other woman. Inside you, you know. And it frightens you. What you feel frightens you. I know this isn't easy, we've known each other a short time. I want to give you better words, but I— I'll get your bags."

Then he was moving out into the night. Uneasy with her tumbling emotions, with the way her body ached for Alexi's, Jessica closed the open windows and the door to the deck. She opened the bathroom that bore only Alexi's scent, but was definitely created to please a woman—the huge footed bathtub sat next to a giant window that would overlook the ocean. A circle of pipe ran high above the tub and from it, a shower curtain pushed aside. The showerhead was well above average height, indicating the remodeling had taken Alexi's height into consideration. Rolls of thick towels stood in a basket and a large shell filled with Willow's fragrant soaps sat on the stool near the bathtub. Plush area rugs ran over the white tile-like linoleum, softening the room. A vanity spread beneath a wide mirror topped by soft lights. *It's for you,* Alexi had said.

Was he that certain of her? That she would come to him?

Or were the small foil squares on the vanity meant for another woman? Did they belong to another woman?

He came through the door, raindrops glittering on his bare shoulders, and placed her luggage on a big wide chair. He turned off the bald electric light overhead and lit a match, taking it to the candles on the table. The flames flickered, throwing his tall shadow against the wall.

Jessica held her breath as Alexi walked to her. "Take off your coat," he ordered in a whisper so raw and powerful that it rocked the room.

Her hand shot out to grip his jeans' waistband, anchoring her fears, and Alexi nodded slowly. He leaned down to kiss her, gently seeking and rekindling the heat they'd just ignited in her car.

"I brought my own," she whispered against his lips.

"Mmm. What?"

"Protection. Yours? Hers? In the bathroom?"

"They are mine, and if you came prepared…then you came for me." The statement was rich with pleasure as Alexi began to remove her coat. "That means you want me bad."

"Or you want me."

"True. If I'm going to get you out of this coat and into my bed, you'll have to let go of my jeans…. Or you can take them off."

When she slowly unsnapped his jeans, her fingers trembled as she pulled down the zipper, only to find his arousal, hot and full, cradled within her hand. Satiny and hard, it burned her skin, and Alexi's shudder caused her to look down, to stare in wonder at what she held in her hand…what would enter her body—

She drew back suddenly and stared at Alexi. She wasn't afraid with him; she only felt the waves of desire pound at her, pressing into her, gliding, penetrating her defenses, tearing away everything but the primitive need to take him.

Jessica let her raincoat fall away and held her breath, reveling in the way Alexi looked at her body. "Come here," he ordered, without moving. "To me."

"I'm already here."

"I meant closer." He bent slowly to lift her and carry her as he had before. But this time he settled her into his bed.

Alexi removed his jeans and eased into the big bed, turning on his side to study her. Jessica smoothed his damp hair and tried to relax as his hand moved over her, caressing gently, seeking entrance to her body. "You're going to know that you're mine before morning comes," he whispered against her lips.

"Or you're going to know that you're never going to forget me," she answered unevenly as his open mouth dragged softly across her skin to find her breast, locking to it gently. At the first tug of his lips, the tender play of his teeth and tongue, Jessica closed her eyes and fought the building pleasure within her.

With a rough sound, Alexi turned from her, reaching into the nightstand drawer. With her hand on his taut back, Jessica murmured, "I want to fit it—"

"Not this time," he stated rawly, and she understood his impatience because her own body was burning, aching.

When Alexi came back into her arms, they lay facing each other. She stroked that hard, taut body—his cheek, his throat, the width of his shoulder and to his hip, then across that rippling belly and up to the rough texture of that wedge of hair.

Her fingertip prowled slowly downward and Alexi sucked in air, but didn't look away from her as she circled his navel lightly. In the shadows he smiled softly at her. "Take me. This time, you lead."

She'd been taken roughly by another man, and Alexi's soft order had surprised her, giving her the power she'd never had....

Jessica caught him tight with her arms and circled his leg with hers, lightly pulling Alexi until he followed her guidance, resting over her. His kisses continued, a magical seduction that made it so easy for her to take him inside to complete the lock of their bodies.

This was lovemaking, she thought, surprised at the gentle flow, the seeking kisses, the heat within her.

But not enough, her body told her fiercely, and she began to move desperately beneath him.

Before she could catch her passion, restrain it, enjoy the pleasure slowly, the heat and hunger rose and demanded more. Jessica feverishly pitted herself against Alexi's strength, unable to pause, to rest, only to take— At her breasts Alexi's lips burned, his body locking, tormenting hers by drawing away, but Jessica knew deep within her that he was claiming her and that she'd never forget the cup of his hands beneath her hips, lifting her—

Breathing hard, fighting Alexi and herself, Jessica fought and welcomed the oncoming tide of pleasure that burst over her.

Against her, Alexi's heart raced, his body pulsing within hers, hers constricting faster and faster. Above her, he looked starkly primitive, fierce, foreign and yet familiar, a male counterpart to her passion.

Jessica forced her fingers to relax on his body, aware that she had demanded everything so real it was starkly primitive, as if nothing else mattered.

The fire crackled lightly as Alexi seemed to struggle to breathe, those fierce, glittering eyes studying her, his fingers stroking her hair across the pillow. He smiled gently, easing back a strand from her damp cheek. "You look stunned."

"Don't leave me," she whispered, closing her lids against everything but the feel of his weight upon her, in her, the stroking of his hands. With care, Alexi lowered his head to rest beside hers, his kisses flowing along her cheek.

Holding him anchored gave her comfort, because Jessica's mind churned, shocked by the passion she'd never experienced, by her own needs...by the freedom Alexi had given her to explore—

"You're thinking too hard," Alexi whispered against her cheek, nuzzling it to find her ear.

She turned to meet his kiss and stayed awhile to enjoy it before she moved against him once more, taking what she wanted, seeing if the first time was only in her mind—it wasn't.

Then, exhausted and stunned and oddly complete, Jessica lay snuggled against him, her head on his shoulder. She hadn't expected Alexi's tenderness, the way he held her against him later, wrapping them both in the blankets.

She awoke to him kissing her, stroking her. Dreamlike, she opened to him, found slow, melting pleasure with him and slept again.

When she awoke again, aching slightly and stretching within the warm cocoon of the blankets, she listened to the shower. Morning prowled around the heavy drapes over the windows and Jessica struggled with how to meet Alexi on this new plane. She knew exactly what had happened; it had been her choice, her need. What could she say? Should she leave now to avoid embarrassment?

She drew the sheet close against her as he opened the bathroom door. Alexi walked naked into the room while rubbing his hair with a towel.

His dark, sensual look at her told Jessica that nothing would erase the night and what had passed, and that now they were lovers, a man and a woman, starting a new day and a new relationship. "You rested well?" he asked formally.

"Very well. Thank you."

"Take your bath. I'll make breakfast," Alexi said as if they had been lovers forever, comfortable with awakening to each other.

He drew on his jeans and Jessica thought how sleek and beautiful he was, muscles sliding beneath that tanned skin— and then she found Alexi staring at her, his hands on his hips, daring her—

"A bath would be lovely." Bracing herself, Jessica threw back the covers; she could equal his sophistication. Head high, she walked naked into the bathroom and closed the door. She leaned against it and shook her head, wondering how she could be so bold.

But when she turned to the mirror, she saw another woman, one tousled and warm and uncertain.

The door opened and Alexi moved behind her. He dropped her overnight bag on the floor and his hands came up to cup her breasts, his head lowering to hers. In the mirror, his stare was bold and possessive, and darkened when her hands came to rest over his and her emerald wedding rings caught the light from the window.

His thumbs teased her nipples. "Tell me why the way we made love surprised you."

"It was so…primitive. I came after you like—"

"Like a woman who knows what she wants," Alexi finished, and moved to draw her bath.

When he turned, she was holding a towel in front of her, trying to adjust to this man, this new, baldly real situation. And Alexi wasn't making it easy or allowing her to retreat. While the water ran, he sat on the edge of the tub, silhouetted by the ocean view behind him. "Willow tells me you like this bubble bath," he said, pouring a liquid into the water.

Layers of steam and the sound of running water filled the room as Alexi looked at her, stirring the bathwater with his hand.

Her body seemed to simmer, hungry for his. Jessica wanted him even now, even after three times during the night!

A woman who had planned and controlled every day in her life, Jessica shivered and fought for a grasp on the morning. She couldn't look away from the dark sensuality, the recognition in Alexi's eyes. She felt herself heating, opening, waiting—and shivered again with the intensity of sensations, both physical and emotional, that she'd never known.

His gaze slowly, possessively, took in her body, then he rose and walked past her. "Enjoy your bath."

"You said this was for me. What did you mean?"

"I saw the tub and I thought of you in it. I asked Willow what she thought you'd like for soaps and women's things—"

Alarmed that her friend might be hurt, Jessica reached out to grasp his arm. "Willow? Alexi, she's half in love with you. She'll be terribly hurt."

Alexi smoothly took her hand and raised it to his lips. "I told her that you were coming to stay with me. She seemed pleased."

"You shouldn't have told her that."

His thumb cruised slowly across her sensitized lower lip. "Are you ashamed of what has happened between us?"

"I don't want Willow to be hurt. She's my only and best friend."

Alexi traced her hair, his fingertip following a strand on her bare shoulder. "She loves you. She's worried about you, about Howard pushing you. She almost gave her blessing."

Jessica placed her hand over the large one prowling down over the towel to cup her breast. "I've been handling Howard for a long time. Willow knows that."

His eyes locked with hers and narrowed dangerously. "Yes, but now I'm in the picture, aren't I?"

She'd been possessed—owned and used—before. But Alexi's statement didn't offend her, because their lovemaking held layers of tenderness and comfort, and she had possessed him equally. "Definitely. Did you find out anything about who might be bothering Willow?"

Alexi frowned slightly. "No. She isn't talking. But with you around, she might. I just called her to tell her that you'd probably be by later today. I told her you spent the night here."

"Alexi! You shouldn't have done that."

"She didn't seem surprised. I'm hoping you'll spend more." With that, he closed the door softly behind him.

Jessica had just adjusted to her privacy and her thoughts when Alexi strolled in carrying two cups of coffee. He smiled briefly as she sank lower into the mounds of bubbles and then handed a cup to her. "You'll have to sit up to drink that."

The dark, rich brew smelled like heaven. He smelled delicious, and he was grinning like a boy tormenting a girl. "You're not going to ask me to leave, are you?"

"Of course not."

"Of course. You're only hiding your body beneath the sudsy water because you're not shy, right? Tell me how it is that no man has seen your body," he ordered suddenly, surprising her. "Tell me why you have been married twice and are still so tight inside. Tell me why you are surprised at how your body reacts, at your own needs. Tell me why you blush when you think of how we made love."

Intimate talk, lovers' talk in the early morning, frightening talk, which could reveal too much…. "I want to understand," Alexi added softly, watching her.

"I—I'd rather not," she said quietly, avoiding his stare as she sipped her coffee and stared out the window. "This view is magnificent."

"Yes, it is." Alexi's voice was deep and uneven, and when she forced herself to turn back to him, their sexual hunger leaped into life, quivering on the steamy layers in the room.

Alexi stood and walked over to the tub. His gaze lowered to her breasts, surrounded by bubbles. "Very beautiful. But if I don't leave now, I'll be in that tub with you."

"There's not room."

"You should see your face. You're shocked, Mrs. Sterling—come out when you're ready." Alexi chuckled softly as he closed the door, leaving her alone.

He was hungry for Jessica even now, Alexi thought as he placed a platter of bacon, eggs and toast onto the table.

Jessica's slow, careless stroll into the bathroom must have cost her, because she must be aching and because she was definitely shaken by her own desire. She'd fought her passion, shaking within his arms, and yet it had risen out of her fiercely, demanding and hungry and perfectly matching his own needs.

The woman was new to lovemaking, to enjoying it, to the pleasure they'd shared, and he had taken her three times!

Alexi silently promised himself to be very careful of her today, fearful of frightening her away. Jessica was shy of him yet. When she looked at his body earlier, the hunger was there, but also uncertainty. Her lashes had lowered and the blush rising up her cheeks was too revealing. She'd pulled the sheet to her breasts, covering herself; he had been tempted to come back to her, to draw away that sheet and kiss that long, soft body beneath, to make her sigh and shake and—her soft cries echoed within him, his body hard now, though he would resist.

He would give Jessica time to adjust to— She still loved her husband, and it would not do to have him in bed with them.

Alexi didn't like his jealousy of the man who had married Jessica, who had given her everything.

His pride seemed to rise up, choking him when he'd thought his old wounds had healed. When he sensed Jessica had come into the living room, he turned to her. "When you are in my bed, there will be no other man between us."

Those green eyes widened with shock. Clearly unprepared for his harsh demand, Jessica stepped back. Her hair was down, softly framing her face, gleaming in rich shades of chestnut. She wore designer jeans and her feet were bare—the pedicure probably more expensive than he could imagine. But she'd chosen to wear his flannel shirt and that eased his uncertainty about her love for her husband.

That haughty look was there, the independent woman with an obvious chip on her shoulder. "Terms, Alexi?"

He lifted an eyebrow and reminded her, "You came to me last night. A man can assume certain things."

"Tell me that wasn't an invitation you served me in Seattle."

Tit for tat, a fighter moving in to protect herself. Alexi admired that, the woman who had chosen him above other men—because it was obvious that Jessica hadn't been sexually active. He enjoyed the way she shifted her head away from his prowling finger, how she stood as he flicked open the shirt to reveal her breasts, to smooth the slightly reddened patches his stubble had caused. "Do they hurt?"

"Do you?"

"But I am not soft and sweet and tender." He cupped her breast and watched that sensual heat leap to those green eyes, darkening them.

"Stop testing me."

"But I have to. Just as you are testing me. It is what we are about—challenges—is it not? I like you wearing my shirt."

"You just have to have it all, don't you? Okay, I'll give it to you. I'm sensitized a little, here and there. This was loose enough to wear without a bra. The lace only—"

"Can breakfast wait?" he murmured against her cheek.

"Can you?" Jessica returned as her arms lifted to circle him and her lips parted for the intimate fit of his....

"Hand that board up to me," Alexi ordered from the rafters over Jessica's head.

At eleven o'clock that morning, she was uneasy with their new relationship. He could feel her circling him, weighing the heat of the storm against the softer moments they'd shared. Her eyes avoided his, and she'd eased away from his body when he passed too close. Jessica was definitely as aware of him as he was of her.

She'd put on her makeup as though she was placing her shields between them, withdrawing back into her control where she could understand and safely schedule and predict.

Alexi had started to work on the roof, bracing it from inside, his work giving him an escape from his emotions. Would she stay the day? Would she stay the night? The week?

He looked down at Jessica and found that mysterious quiet look in those dark green eyes. Was she frightened of what had happened between them? Was she leaving? "Is the lady corporate executive above a little manual labor?" he attempted to tease with a smile.

"I've done my share."

She lifted the short, premeasured board he had pointed to and took a few rungs up the ladder, pausing to hand it up to Alexi. He placed his hand over hers and asked the question troubling him: "Are you staying?"

Her expression was guarded. "I'm going to talk with Willow now. I have to know that she is safe."

"She is."

He lifted the board away and Jessica frowned. "How do you know that Willow is safe, Alexi?"

He shoved the board into place, a support for the old boards, and pounded nails into it. Jessica had moved up the ladder and stood on it, staring at him. "You are a very frustrating man, Alexi Stepanov. Are you going to tell me or not?"

She'd placed her hair into that prim knot, straight back from her face. Dressed now in expensive navy sports slacks and matching jacket, she had settled down earlier to work at her laptop on the kitchen table. He'd heard the ring of her cell phone, her voice muffled. "Who just called you?" Alexi asked.

"I run a business, you know."

"Ah. Howard."

"Yes." The flash of her eyes and Jessica's one word said she didn't want his interference. Too bad, Alexi decided. He was taking the rights of a lover to protect his own.

"Get out of here," he said lightly. "That's what you want to do, isn't it? Leave? Pack up and go, then. We're both adults. There's no need to try to make nice."

He didn't need to look at Jessica to feel her response to his challenge. Alexi could feel her bristle in the cold air between them.

"I thought you Stepanov boys were supposed to be easygoing. But you are definitely a mountain of trouble."

Alexi looked down at her. "Make up your mind. Either you want me—what I am—or you don't."

"Your bruises are showing, Alexi."

"Maybe. Either you stay or not. Either you come back or you don't."

"This is some morning after," she muttered, and tossed a small piece of wood at him.

Alexi moved his arm, deflecting the wood. He'd thought about flowers and breakfast in bed. At another time, when his edges weren't so raw, terrified that she'd walk away from whatever might grow between them, he might have been less harsh. A wealthy woman, Jessica was used to more, more than he could give her.

And he couldn't settle for less than what they could have—"You can't make it here, Jessica. There's no way you can give up everything you have and lower yourself to a working man's life—my life."

"I know what you're doing, Alexi. You want me to commit to you right now. You're challenging me. And you really think I'll walk, don't you?"

"The choice is yours. I want you here, with me. And I'm not sneaking up to the resort to visit your suite when you drop in now and then.'' Maybe his pride was showing—or his fear—but pushing Jessica into a semi-commitment was something he needed now. Uncomfortable with his insecurity, Alexi knew what he was challenging Jessica to do—to overturn her entire life to stay with him, a man who had little to offer. ''If you want to keep tabs on Willow, on whatever her problem is, you'll have to do it yourself. Let me know what you decide.''

Then to soften his fear, to reassure himself and to give Jessica something to balance during her day, Alexi reached down to cradle the nape of her neck. He watched her eyes darken, felt the sensual heat stir in the shadowy cold air between them. ''Come here,'' he whispered.

The resistance to his order was there in the stiffness of her body. She was a woman who chose her own path—would she choose him?

Then she took two more steps up the ladder. That encouraged Alexi, and he bent down slightly. ''Come here,'' he whispered again, and feared he was pushing his luck.

Jessica's next step took her to a level where their lips met and played and warmed. ''I thought you were civilized, Stepanov, or trying to be,'' she whispered, and caught his bottom lip with her teeth.

He smiled lightly and his tongue traced her upper lip. ''Only when I have to be.''

Her lips opened and his tongue instantly slipped inside. Their eyes met, so close he could see himself in the darkness of hers. The slight suction of her mouth caused his body to harden instantly.

Jessica leaned a fraction away, studying him. She licked her lips and tilted her head, those dark green eyes heavy-lidded and sultry. ''I could make you beg.''

The taunt was sexual, playful, and Alexi delighted in this feminine woman set to torment him. ''Try it. Now.''

Her shocked expression pleased him and Alexi couldn't help grinning.

''You're overconfident, Stepanov,'' Jessica murmured. ''Someone needs to take you down.''

''Try.''

She shook her head and Alexi could feel the heat in her, that need to meet his challenges. She snapped her fingers. "I could seduce you in a minute. Just like that."

He grinned, enjoying the intimate, playful rivalry between them. "Try."

"It's cold outside and you're sweaty. You look fizzed. What's wrong?" Willow asked anxiously as Jessica entered her shop.

"I've been running. I do work on keeping in shape, you know." Jessica regretted her sharp reply, an aftermath to fighting her instincts to climb that ladder and wipe the smile— rather, change Alexi's expression to one of that dark hunger.

But then that would have just tripped her own, and they would be back in bed—or the first flat surface or— Jessica blinked with an unexpected thought: Alexi could support her weight; he'd just carried her into the house and he'd carried her to bed.

When he'd looked down at her and said that one word, "Try," she almost did, her body warming and softening and aching for his.

It was all about sex and testing each other's limits, nothing more. Alexi was a tall, fascinating challenge and he knew it. He knew just how to test her, pushing for more.

Jessica held her smile inside, where she was warm and happy and feeling like taking Alexi down and— *All she had to do was to circle him sensually, find his weakness and go for him, and then they'd see about "Try."*

Her legs were shaking—either from her hard run along the beach or thinking about Alexi's demands, pushing her to the limit and leaving her exhausted, clinging, sated and smiling against his damp shoulder. She'd never felt so complete, her body blending with his, as if he were the other part of her. How could a man be so tender, soothing her later? How could he be wrapped in his own demanding hunger and yet put hers first?

Jessica caught Willow's puzzled expression. "I'm sorry, Willow. I've got things on my mind. What were you saying?"

Willow's eyebrows rose and behind the glint of her small glasses, her eyes sparkled with humor. "Things on your mind like Alexi Stepanov? That dreamboat? So you spent the night there? Tell all. I'll put the teakettle on. I've never seen you blush before, Jessica."

Jessica leveled a look at Willow, who was studying her with interest, as if noting every minute change.

She ran her fingertip over the small strawberry-shaped soaps on display with others, all placed in ceramic clam shells and sealed in plastic. Was it that evident? The hours spent making love with Alexi? "It was only because the weather conditions were bad. My car stalled."

"Uh-huh. Like I believe that," Willow said, leading the way back to her apartment. "I know what I'd do if I could catch that guy. I'd nail him on the spot."

Jessica shivered, remembering how Alexi had watched her bathe...how those blue eyes had stroked her body beneath the sudsy water. That dark, contemplative, hungry look brought to life emotions she hadn't experienced, and she feared trusting them.

Once in her kitchen, Willow ran water into the kettle, put it on the flame and turned to Jessica. Willow leaned back against her kitchen counter and studied her friend. "I've known you too well for you to put one over on me. You had sex with him and liked it—this, after not being touched by a man since your teenage marriage. He's got you all steamed up—a man like Alexi would do that to a woman he wanted. And he'd make life pretty darned difficult for that woman, too. Now you're running because you're frustrated and don't know how to handle yourself, or what to do next, and you want to go to him and tell him all that, but you don't know how to give yourself over—to trust anyone but me. Is that about it?"

"Sex? You think I had sex with Alexi? Am I wearing a label or something?" Willow had perfectly described Jessica's problems. She studied Willow, who had often spoken about Alexi, how nice he was. "He's...interesting. Are you interested in him, Willow?"

"He's been around, in the shop and at the resort," Willow

stated cautiously. "Alexi seems interested in me. I hope that doesn't bother you. I wouldn't want my best friend to feel… well, jealous. Do you? I mean, just because you had sex with him doesn't mean that—"

"Of course not."

When Willow grinned, Jessica pushed away that slight burning emotion that she wouldn't call jealousy; Alexi might want another woman, and there was no lasting commitment between them.

Or was there? Her senses told her that their bond as lovers went deeper. Jessica sipped the tea Willow had just poured. Her plan to have Alexi investigate the danger to Willow may have backfired.

Or Alexi could genuinely be interested in Willow.

Jessica's body tightened, remembering Alexi's fierce possession. "If he is interested, he's a darned good—"

"What, Jessica?" Willow asked.

"Nothing." She noted the cardboard taped over Willow's window. It was new; the other broken window was in the shop. "Did you ever find out who broke the window?"

Willow shrugged, but she'd turned her telltale face away from Jessica. "Kids, probably. Probably threw a rock and it accidentally hit my window. They were probably too scared to come tell me."

Concerned for her friend, Jessica placed her hand on Willow's. "Willow, I'm worried. You said someone was calling, breathing heavily. You're here alone. You could be in danger."

"It was probably someone who just got the wrong number."

"And took a few minutes breathing heavily? I don't think so."

"Jessica, they dialed the wrong number, and when they heard my voice, it took them a moment to regroup. That's all."

"It's someone you know, isn't it? Someone is threatening you and—"

"And I do not want trouble," Willow finished briskly. She turned to Jessica, studying her over the rims of her small glasses. "We both know that Alexi has only one woman on his mind. Last week, when you were in Seattle, he had the lonesomest look. And he's the first man to interest you. Are you going to grab this chance or not? Does Howard know? I do not like that guy. He's a bully. You should separate completely from him.''

"I can't. He's Robert's son. Robert asked me to protect Sterling Stops, but also to understand that he'd never given Howard the father he needed. Robert felt guilty about that, and I promised him that I'd watch out for Howard.''

On a visit to Sterling Stops' corporate office, Willow had experienced firsthand Howard's jealousy, his anger and his need to possess Jessica. A simple lunch date between friends had infuriated him—especially when he invited himself and Jessica preferred Willow's company over his. Alarmed that Howard could be stalking Willow, Jessica asked, "Has Howard called you? Has he come here?''

Willow's expression tightened and she crossed her arms, leveling a look at Jessica. "Honey, that was over four months ago. He knows you and I are close and wanted me to get you to play ball on some deal or another. I kicked him out. He made a pass at me—it was like, 'gee whiz, she's a woman, and I've got some spare time. I'm doing her a favor.' Look, dear heart, I detest the guy and I can protect myself against someone like him.''

Infuriated at the lengths Howard would go, Jessica placed her cup into the sink. "You should have told me. I'll see that Howard doesn't bother you again.''

"I can handle myself—with some jerk like him anyway. He was limping when he left. I believe his crotch was hurting. He won't be back. But what about you? Are you going to stop him from bothering you, too?''

"I've been stopping it for years.'' But Alexi had just upped the ante because Howard would consider him to be a poacher.

"So you spent the night with Alexi and now you're set to go right back where you were—killing yourself with work and guilt. That's what you plan to do, isn't it?'' Willow asked. "And if I didn't care, I just might let you do that. But I do care, and I want you to take some time to deal with what you need as a person, as a woman—to find yourself and what you deserve. You do not owe anyone anything. You've already paid too much—first of all to that family, and then to that idiot you married before that. I know you loved Robert, but now it's time to move on—and if I weren't your friend and didn't love you dearly, I wouldn't be telling you that it's time to deal with your life and your feelings."

Willow paused to take a deep breath as if unloading a huge burden. "He came after you, didn't he? And you came here to see him, didn't you? Gee whiz, it doesn't take a brainiac to figure out there is something cooking between you. Go for it, Jess."

"Are you finished?" Jessica asked, shocked because Willow had always been so careful not to voice her very definite opinions about her friend's life.

"No. There's this." Willow stepped close and hugged and rocked Jessica. As if firmly resolved, Willow stepped back. "I needed that. Because I'm terribly afraid."

Jessica took her friend's hand and smoothed a tightly waving strand back from her forehead. "I told you. I'll see that you're protected. I'm not leaving here without some safeguard in place for you."

Willow's fingers tightened on Jessica's. "Jess, I'm a busybody and shouldn't interfere, but we're best friends. Aren't we?"

"Of course. How did you interfere? The soap you sent to the office? It was lovely. My secretary wants to order more for her friends—"

"I had good motives. Don't hate me."

"But I could never hate you. You're the only person I've ever trusted with how I feel, with my life—"

"You might hate me after this," Willow muttered as if to herself. After taking a deep breath, her words rushed from her. "I set this up. You said that your relationship with Robert—wasn't sexual, though you loved him. Now you seem to be locked in to that business. I knew you'd stay in that office, working yourself to death, and that deadbeat, Howard, would be leering at you. Someday, when you're tired and down, he'll probably catch you and—"

Willow paused and looked at her wristwatch. "Oh, shoot. I was supposed to pick up Patience to take her to the clinic and then drop by to take Frank to the grocery store, and then go back and pick up Patience. Oh, wait a minute, before Patience, I was supposed to… It's my day to shuttle everyone around and I forgot. I was worried about you and a shipment of supplies was due and—"

Jessica placed her fingertip in the center of Willow's forehead, effectively stopping the flow of Willow's schedule. Jessica sensed she wasn't going to like whatever was coming next in her friend's plot to get her to Amoteh. "Let's get back to you worrying about me not managing my own life. I was tired and rundown and Howard was bothering me…. And?"

Willow threw up her hands and shook her head. "I think you're a great match for Alexi, and you weren't taking my hints so I had to act. I knew you'd come here and stay, to protect me. Since I played summer theater—"

"I knew I wasn't going to like this."

"You're looking all dark and mad… Like when you think something isn't my business, but it's bothering you—like resolving your family stuff—and I think you should get it out and talk about it…. And besides, it might actually be true that someone is stalking me. But it isn't…. Okay, well. My motives were well-intended. Just don't hate me…. Oh, I just hate it when you get that scrunched-up look like when I paid that guy to dance with you—I really did think he was a good match for you and you needed to feel like a woman instead of a machine…. Um, would you like me to make you some fudge? I'll cancel everything and close the shop. It's going to rain today. We can watch movies and eat chocolate and—"

"You faked danger to yourself because you knew I'd get involved with Alexi? You did that? Does Alexi know? *Does Alexi know?*"

Willow's hands raised to rub circles on her temples and she frowned at Jessica from between her little fingers. "I knew you'd get all worked up. I can't do everything, you know. I'm supposed to give this little talk to some ladies on retreat at the Amoteh about soap-making. One of their grandmothers actually made her own and she's basically called me out to prove that I'm a fake, that real soap-making is done with fat, lye and a kettle. It's a duel, Jessica, and I have to turn up. The ladies are afraid they'll fall in the mud, so I have to go to them. I stand to get some big orders out of them. I forgot about the appointments I had to transport the elderly, and you're just going to have to help me out.''

"Oh, I am, am I?''

"Yes, you are. Because you're my friend and I'm yours, and I know that you had good sex last night, because you're glowing.'' Willow picked up a pad and pencil and started sketching a map.

She handed it to Jessica. "You'll help me, won't you, Jess? Please, please, please? I love you, Jessie, and the marked Xs are pickups with the names and times,'' she singsonged.

"Give me that and never call me Jessie again,'' Jessica ordered without anger as she snatched the map. How could she possibly be angry with a friend who had given her so much, who was almost the sister she'd wanted for a lifetime?

Jessica leaned away from Willow's kiss on her cheek and said, "Okay, but you're pushing it. But don't think that I'm done with you, or with Alexi. I'm not happy that you set this up, and if he has any idea of what you've done, I'm going to teach him a lesson.''

Seven

$\mathbf{A}$t seven o'clock, the night was quiet and moonlit outside the Stepanov Furniture Shop. Unable to stay in his home and pursued by images of Jessica, by her scent, Alexi had come to work on the desk. He had started it during the week Jessica was in Seattle. Now, he didn't want to go home to find her gone, so he had stayed away.

He ran his hand over the smooth unfinished walnut of the small secretary desk. In the plain, sturdy style of Stepanov Furniture, the desk was large enough for a laptop and a small printer. The cubbyholes and narrow drawer would serve well for necessities.

He'd designed the functional desk to suit a woman like Jessica—strong, intelligent, elegant, confident and smooth to the touch, to enjoy touching. The reddish grain running through the dark walnut reminded him of her hair—

Alexi traced the wood with his finger and thought of how her hair had looked, vivid against her pale skin. He hadn't seen Jessica since that morning and ached to hold her in his arms, to let her scent comfort him, arouse him—

Something else brewed between them, a tenderness and intimacy that seemed fresh and clean. Could he trust that bond?

Was Jessica still emotionally married to her deceased husband? Did her heart still belong to him?

Alexi turned off the sander and began using sandpaper. He was usually a patient man, but now he waited anxiously for each word of Jessica. He needed his hands busy, anything to distract him from how Jessica's silky skin had felt beneath his touch, those soft purrs, the rise of her hips to meet his....

Willow had called, serving him a warning that Jessica might be detained a bit by helping the elderly run errands—but Alexi was definitely on Jessica's hit list.

Jessica hadn't left Amoteh; her BMW had been collected by Willow. Mikhail had said that Willow had parked the expensive vehicle in the resort's parking lot and had delivered her soap program to the ladies' retreat group. Willow had been thrilled with the orders she had taken, and she had mentioned that Jessica was delivering the elderly to different appointments in Amoteh.

Alexi grimly pushed the sandpaper across the already-smooth top of the secretary desk. It couldn't compare to Jessica's elegant office desk, but he wanted to give her something unique, made by his own hands and heart.

The door to the furniture shop crashed open and Fadey walked in, grinning and bold, carrying a picnic basket. "My wife, your aunt, she worries for you, little boy. She sent you food."

Jarek and Mikhail followed him inside, and the men placed the containers they carried onto the workbench. They stripped off their coats and began setting the food out.

"So you're hiding out here. Jessica is hunting you," Mikhail stated as he began to slice his wife's freshly baked bread. "She came to the Amoteh and used the complimentary business suite to make calls."

Alexi frowned slightly; he knew his cousin was baiting him and he wouldn't be too anxious to ask about Jessica.

Would Jessica want to stay with Alexi? She was a powerful woman and he was asking her to stay with him, assist him and live in basic conditions. Maybe Jessica was right—he could be punishing her for the damage another woman had done.

Jarek opened the pie container and cut the pie, sliding a big piece onto a plate that Fadey had placed beside him. Fadey tapped another plate, indicating he wanted a piece of the pie. Mikhail took the slice that Jarek had placed onto a plate, and began eating.

"That is *my* wife's cherry pie," Jarek stated darkly.

With the air of an older brother challenging a younger one, Mikhail asked, "So?"

Jarek frowned at Mikhail and placed a slice onto another plate. "Jessica has been at the Seagull's Perch and at Willow's."

Alexi breathed deeply; he knew his cousins well. One anxious word about Jessica and they would be teasing him.

Was Jessica saying her goodbyes to her friend? Alexi pretended he wasn't listening. He tossed the sandpaper aside and picked up the pie pan, stuck a fork into the remainder of the cherry pie and started eating. "The house is coming along. I got a good section of the roof braced up. By the time the weather is better, we can shingle."

"Shakes might be better for that house. It rambles on too much to be an upright saltbox design and it isn't quite ranch style. But we have time to think about roofing. We could make the shakes here," Mikhail noted, always the practical businessman.

"But did she like the bathroom? Women like kitchens and bathrooms," Jarek stated with experience.

Alexi thought of Jessica soaking in her bubble bath, the way she leaned her head back against the rolled towel and closed her eyes—that little sigh of pleasure. His pleasure was in just looking at her. He placed the pie aside. "She liked it."

"That's what I heard from my wife. Jessica and Ellie talked briefly," Mikhail said softly. Just another nudge in the cousins' teasing, Alexi decided.

Then he gave in to his curiosity. He tried to shield his excitement. "Did she say anything, Mikie?"

"You know I don't like that nickname." Mikhail shrugged and answered obliquely, "Woman talk. Things."

"Like what, specifically?" Then Alexi caught the knowing smiles passing between Mikhail and Jarek. "Stop," Alexi ordered darkly. "There are things that I know about you, cousins, that your wives would like to know."

He could still taste Jessica, still smell that exotic, feminine scent, still want her…. *Was she gone? Would she think of him tonight as she lay in her luxurious bedroom in Seattle?*

Fadey circled the little desk. "Good. Good, clean, sturdy. A woman would like this. You put the same hardware on it as what Mikhail used for Ellie's sewing machine. A little touch to please a woman."

"Jessica delivered groceries to Mrs. Maloney and took a prescription to Tiny Morales on Willow's behalf. Looks like she's keeping busy. Ryan had to help her jump-start Willow's old van. She asked him about regular transportation services for the elderly or housebound in Amoteh."

"Neighbors usually help. Willow seems to have taken charge of anyone who doesn't have help." Alexi slathered butter over a slice of warm, thick bread. "There's nothing to keep Jessica here—"

The door swung open and Jessica, a worn, knitted scarf around her head, covered in mud, stepped inside. She slammed the door shut. Her eyes locked on Alexi and narrowed dangerously. "Stepanov, I've been looking all over for you—"

"Which one?" Jarek asked, smothering another smile.

"I smell food." Jessica frowned and she sniffed delicately. Obviously her hunt had been sidetracked.

She stared at the container of stew that Fadey had just placed on the workbench. "Can I have some of that?"

While Mikhail gallantly helped her out of her coat and seated her, Jarek began placing food on the door across two sawhorses that served as a table. Alexi leaned back against the workbench and folded his arms across his chest. He didn't like feeling vulnerable and uncertain.

He studied the tie-dyed T-shirt over her long-sleeved, expensive sweater and the love beads around her throat, an indication that she had visited Ed and Bliss. Willow had said Jessica knew about the deception and would be coming to question him. The option was Alexi's: he could either deny that he knew Willow was faking danger to herself, or he could admit his suspicions.

When Jessica began devouring the food placed in front of her, Jarek waved his hand in a low, sweeping invitation for Alexi to sit next to her. Fadey, Mikhail and Jarek stood back against the workbench, leisurely enjoying their food. They watched Alexi ease into the chair next to Jessica.

Alexi frowned at the other men; they looked as if they were set to enjoy good theater. "So how was your day?" he asked Jessica as casually as he could. *Are you staying here? With me?*

He buttered the warm bread and placed it on her plate. Jessica was still eating quickly. Alexi ate a few bites from his plate and then asked, "Did you eat today?"

"No time," she said around a mouthful of stew.

He unwound the long, knitted scarf from her throat and touched one of her braids. "That's a new hairstyle."

"Mrs. Olaf was showing me how she braided her daughter's hair. I mentioned I had mine braided as a girl and, naturally… It's called French braiding. It's very tight. I may be squinting. There are little tight strands catching at the nape of my neck. I just haven't had the time to undo it." She turned her attention to the food. "Gee, this is good."

Alexi eased away the elastic hair band from one braid; his fingers began to loosen Jessica's hair from its confinement. At a sound, he turned to see his cousins and uncle all grinning.

"It is really tight," Alexi stated defensively, because he wanted to tend Jessica, to hold her, and they knew exactly how he felt.

"Got to go," Mikhail stated abruptly, as though Alexi's gestures reminded him of a task he couldn't wait to do. "Jessica, do you want the resort's housekeeping staff to warm your suite a bit? Maybe ready the fireplace?"

The shop was suddenly heavy with silence. She stopped

spooning stew into her mouth and looked blankly at Alexi. "I haven't had time to think…. I might—''

In that heartbeat, Alexi had everything he'd needed all day—Jessica wanted to be close to him. She'd thought of him through her busy day and she'd needed him. She might want to sort out the facts with Alexi—but she wanted to be held close by him.

"I'll take her home," he said quietly.

Fadey clapped his hands and, with his arm looped through Jarek's, began a brief, stomping, circular dance. He clapped again and grinned. "That's good. You make me happy. You take her home, boy."

"Pop," Mikhail warned quietly when Jessica put her head down, obviously shielding a blush.

"I am only joyful for my brother, Viktor, you know. Not for me," Fadey stated adamantly. Then his eyes lit. It was an expression Alexi had seen when Fadey talked of the grand-children he wanted. "Yes, I am joyful, too. So what, little boy?"

"We're working on it, Pop. Less than two weeks and you'll have another grandchild. Mom says Ellie is in her nesting mood."

Fadey's expression was concerned and almost comically contrite, his shoulders lifted, his hands outstretched in a plea. "But my brother, Viktor, you know. He is younger, but without little ones."

"Uncle," Alexi cautioned quietly. Jessica hadn't seemed to notice the exchange, but Alexi's body tightened almost fiercely as he thought of how they had made love, and the child that could be—a little girl with green eyes and braids. He'd heard of the primitive urge to hold his own child, but he hadn't really experienced that deep need with one special woman.

When Heather was telling him how she had used him to mark time—"until someone better came along"—she'd also included a bare fact that she'd previously hidden. "I wouldn't think of having children. It would ruin my figure."

Alexi studied Jessica's clean-cut profile. She might not want children, either. It didn't really matter now. He knew little about her—except that he ached to hold her, to make love to her.

Mikhail sighed and said his goodbyes. Jessica was still looking down and Alexi couldn't resist running his fingertip over her hot cheek, enjoying that delicious little shiver. "Tired?"

"Very. I have a surprise for you."

"I can't wait."

Her hunger satisfied now, Jessica yawned. When Alexi finished loosening her other braid, her head nodded and her head drooped. She leaned slightly toward Alexi and all his unrest settled into a gentle flow of tenderness for her. He eased her from her chair and into her coat, wrapping the knitted scarf around her head. With a quiet look to Fadey and Jarek, Alexi guided Jessica toward the door.

Jessica awoke in Alexi's bed. Alone, she lay in the heavy warmth of the quilts, inhaling his scent. She ran her hand over his pillow and remembered how he had carried her into the house. When he had placed her on her feet, Jessica had swayed and then leaned fully against him. Alexi had chuckled, the sound deep and rich against her cheek. "It must have been some day."

"I had to jump-start Willow's van. Then I drove it into the nearest garage and had them drop a battery in it. On the trips, someone was baby-sitting their grandchild and the girl was carsick and that wasn't pleasant. Ed and Bliss and I chased their goat. I slid down a hill."

"But did you get the goat?"

Alexi already knew Jessica's answer. "Yes."

She'd fumbled in her pocket, determined to give Alexi her present. "Here. A worry stone from Ed. Bliss is worried about your chakras. She said they have been out of alignment for too long. And I think you need this, too."

Jessica watched the firelight flickering on the ceiling and remembered Alexi's soft, pleased smile as she'd placed her love beads over his head. "Don't worry anymore, Alexi. I've taken care of everything."

"Have you?" he asked, amused as he gently washed her face with a cloth.

The wind howled outside and water dropped from the ceiling into the bucket, but Jessica never felt more safe. She remembered his big, callused, warm hands running gently over her nude body, a comforting gesture that told her she had come home—where she belonged, with Alexi.

Never in her life had she been so safe and cherished. After a childhood of uncertainty and neglect, an immature marriage and her second with Robert—because already ill, Robert had needed protection from his son's greed and cruelty—Jessica had fought to keep him safe, to keep Robert's dream safe.

She stretched and sighed and luxuriated in this tiny moment—before she would tell Alexi what she had done.

And ask him if he knew about Willow's playacting.

Now, turning in his bed alone, Jessica frowned slightly. She realized that the cool sheets beside her body hadn't been warmed by Alexi's. She listened to the slight splashing sounds in the bathroom and reached for her wristwatch, which was lying on the table beside the bed. "Two o'clock is a strange time to be taking a...bath. Hmm. Alexi seems more like a shower man."

She rose slowly and stretched, her whole body aching from the day before—and from Alexi's possession. Her breasts were sensitized, her body aware that it had been shared intimately with Alexi.

He'd gently undressed her—completely—and now with the colder air hitting her naked body, Jessica smiled. Alexi had obviously had his own plans while putting her to bed, but waylaid them because of her exhaustion.

She wasn't exhausted now and a rendezvous with Alexi in that enormous bathtub was too good to ignore. In her lifetime, Jessica never explored her sensuality, and it was now definitely awakening her hunting instincts to seduce a very fascinating man. She glanced in the mirror on the wall and frowned at the tiny waves the tight braids had created in her hair. She used her fingers to soothe the wild tigress-woman look, but nothing would change the way she felt or those shadows of a well-loved woman. It was a new look, softer, more feminine, almost shocking her—a woman who had never really explored her personal needs.

Jessica eased the bathroom door open to find Alexi in the tub, his head leaning back against the top, his eyes closed. His arms rested on the edges of the tub, his long legs extended past the other end. Jessica quietly closed the door and leaned against the wall, admiring Alexi—a ripcord-hard, muscled male, almost savage in his beauty—amid a bubble bath.

"Enjoying yourself?" he asked very softly.

"Yes. Definitely. Are you?"

He moved quickly to grab the edges of the tub and surge to his feet. Tall and tan, with water and soapsuds sliding down his body, he stood in the water, his eyes the shade of frost on the window, pinning Jessica. "You've been a busy girl."

She stared at his fit body. "And you're tan all over."

"Skinny-dipping in a Wyoming creek on a hot day does that." Alexi stepped out of the tub and briskly wiped himself dry. He wrapped a towel around his waist and slashed a cold look at Jessica. "So you thought you'd buy me a present, a nice little toy to keep me busy and happy? And I'm not talking about Ed's worry stone."

He walked out of the bathroom, leaving her breathless and shaken.

Alexi tossed away the towel and glanced at the bathroom door that had just slammed behind him. Apparently Jessica had decided to give herself thinking room.

He took a pair of folded jeans from the laundry basket and tugged them on. Jessica's pale curves, those breasts and hips and long legs, the intriguing V between them, had already stoked the hunger in his body. Her hair had added a sexy new look; her eyes were shadowed and mysterious, almost absorbing him from head to toe. He'd known the taste of her lips, of her skin, of the nipples peaking upon those soft breasts and beneath the bathwater, and his body had stirred, aroused so fiercely that he didn't bother to hide it as he stood.

Her gaze had taken him in, stroking his flesh with heat, even as the water cooled it. He'd almost tugged her to him, taken her as she wanted.

It would all be so easy, to step into what she wanted—to make love—but Alexi's pride wouldn't allow that—

A heartbeat later, the door slammed behind Jessica and she walked across the room toward him. The flannel shirt he'd hung in the bathroom earlier reached her midthigh as she walked to her luggage. She bent to open it, the sound of the zipper ripping through the quiet room. With a disdaining look at Alexi, she crouched to select clothing and then stood, her stare cool and hard.

They'd known each other intimately; she was giving him notice that she could equal him on any level. When she started to walk to the bathroom, Alexi said quietly, "That isn't necessary. I've seen everything."

Jessica paused midstep and straightened her shoulders. With her back to him, she tossed her fresh clothing onto a dresser. She let his shirt fall to the floor and raised her arms to let a soft green lounging gown with long sleeves slide over her body. Then, with her arms folded across her breasts, Jessica said briskly, "Okay, let's have it, Stepanov."

"What, Mrs. Sterling? Sex or a discussion about why you are *not* buying the Seagull's Perch for me?"

"I was going to tell you—"

But Alexi's anger wouldn't wait. "The notes you left on the table were interesting. Was the tavern some little gift of appreciation? A buy-off? What? I called Barney last night while you were sleeping. He said you were thinking of buying and if you did, that you wanted me to take the place on full-time, managing it. He wanted me to know, so I'd have time to get my finances up for a purchase price—he wants to know that his place is going to someone he knows will take care of it. And he prefers me."

When Jessica flinched slightly, Alexi regretted his harshness, but pride drove him on. He lifted her notations on the tavern's profit and loss statements, the amount of the owner's asking price, and slapped the paper next to her laptop. "Let's get this straight right now. You may buy presents for other men. You're not buying me anything."

Those green eyes glinted as she came to tap his chest with her fingertip. "How do you know it's for you, Stepanov?"

Despite his leashed anger, Alexi couldn't help admiring her spirit. "We're lovers. You may call me Alexi. And because we are lovers, you are not buying that tavern. Do you think I'm going to work for you? Did you even think how that would look?"

Jessica's hard stare flickered at that last charge. "No, I didn't. I told you, I had quite the day, starting off with discovering that my best friend was wrangling my life. Willow intimated that she was in danger, knowing full well that I would be looking for ways to protect her—and, gee whiz, she knew me pretty well. I went straight for the best protection available—you."

"Then you made deliveries, chased a goat and got into tentative negotiations for buying the Seagull's Perch and establishing me as manager. I pay my own way, Jessica."

"So do I. And I'm not Heather. You've got a big chip on your shoulder, Stepanov. I meant well. I only moved into a business opportunity and checked it out. Barney had heard that we—that we might be involved, and he said he liked you. And that the tavern is his lifelong baby and he really wanted to pass it on to someone who would take good care of it. That was when I said that you would probably make a good manager. I was going to talk it over with you—and will, when you're not acting as if I'd committed grand larceny. I refuse to be intimidated, by you or anyone else, not at this stage of my life—I was once and I didn't like it."

"Then perhaps you are the one wearing the chip." Alexi flicked his finger against her shoulder.

"Maybe I am. And maybe I know what it is to really want something. That you and I are lovers didn't make a difference."

"People will think—"

Jessica leveled a dark look at him. "You're bigger than that."

"You have a high opinion of me then. If so, you should know that *a man does not like his woman buying expensive presents for him.*"

Her head went back. "You're yelling. Please desist. We are lovers. I admit that. I take responsibility for what I do. But I own myself. To think that my best friend stepped in to arrange my life, to worry me—I still haven't gotten over that, and you knew, didn't you?"

"She used onions to make herself cry. She printed the threatening notes herself. She's been studying crime and stalkers. Yes, I had a good idea she was faking."

His woman. The echo of his previous words stunned him. In his heart he thought of Jessica as his—and himself as hers—not as a possession, but as a softer bond coursing between them. Frustrated, more with himself for not handling the situation better, Alexi reached to fist that soft hair and demand, "You never yell, I suppose."

Her hands shot up to hold his face. "Never. I can control my temper, but you're pushing it, Stepanov."

He leaned his forehead against hers, looking straight into those emerald eyes. "You are a complicated woman."

"No more than you."

He had to shrug and smile at that. "But, observe—I am a man. With a man's pride—"

With his free arm, he jerked her closer, to let her know that she was his, in the soft place in his heart, one he guarded very well. "And a man's desire."

Jessica tensed, her face lifted to his. Those green eyes glittered up at him. "You like this, don't you? This sparring? Challenging me?"

"Yes, because then I see inside you, past what you do not want others to know. Tell me more about you. Tell me what you're struggling so hard to prove."

He tapped her forehead. "I already know that you probably didn't make love with Robert, that yours was a marriage of convenience. You probably loved each other, and with the son he had, he needed you to be the protégée who took care of a business he loved. With the age difference, Robert could have been a father to you, which meant you either lost your own father or you didn't like him…. Something is going on in there and it isn't letting you rest. It's holding you. And you can't let it go.''

"Okay, here's one basic. I like to give gifts. I couldn't once, but now I can afford it. I work hard for my money. Nothing was handed to me, despite what Howard says. I knew you would be upset, but I was only querying about the tavern. I know you are—temperamental…emotional…deeply proud, and wounded. I was going to see what you thought, and that a payment schedule could be—"

"But now? Now that I know?"

"You just have to push, don't you? I've only been here one night and one day, and already I know that I'll never meet anyone as aggravating as you. This is only money, Alexi, not life's blood.''

Alexi had never felt that need before—to strip away everything but the truth and leave it clean and good. And Jessica didn't want herself exposed to him. Too bad. Yesterday his insecurities about Jessica had prowled around him and now, stretched raw with pride, they had to be served. "And you thought to bargain with me? Is that how you handle relationships? Tell me about your first marriage."

"Bargains are made all the time, Stepanov. Good ones that work for both sides. But I see that you're not one to take the easiest road possible to what you want."

"I'll be the judge of that."

Jessica inhaled sharply and pushed back from him. She wrapped her arms around herself and went to look out at the night, the ocean waves catching the moonlight. "You wanted to know about my first marriage. I was young. We were both too young. I wanted to get away from my family. Not all families are like yours, Alexi. My mother wouldn't leave my father, an alcoholic, and life wasn't sweet. But it wasn't reason enough to marry or to have children with Travis—I saw that instantly, if a little late. After the divorce, I started working at whatever I could find, moving up a job at a time. I cut off relations with my family and I moved away. Then I met Robert, when I was managing a Sterling Stops. You know the rest. End of story."

Not all families are like yours, Alexi.... The wound was there, still bleeding, and Alexi ached for her. "So this is what you protect so fiercely—you still think of your family. You still hurt. And you're covering that with a smile-it-doesn't-hurt attitude."

"They didn't miss me. They wanted my paycheck, though. Sometime ago, Howard dug them up and started trouble. Robert was dying and, to keep him in peace, I made arrangements for monthly payments to them. That's the deal—they stay away from me, they get money."

Alexi wanted to go to her, to hold her. But that would be too easy and Jessica clearly didn't want sympathy. She wanted closed doors between them, and Alexi wasn't a man who liked to deal with unexpected shadows. How long had she gone disliking that part of herself that had to survive?

"If Robert was kind to you and someone hurt you, a man, then it would have been Travis?"

Jessica's fingers tightened on her upper arms. "Let's just say that he was young and didn't understand anything past his own needs. He really just didn't understand that women—that sex—wasn't wham-bam. He was raised that way. I don't blame him."

"But you should. Scream," Alexi ordered quietly as he stood and crossed his arms.

She pivoted instantly to him, her expression puzzled. "What did you say?"

"If you have never yelled, then scream. It is good for you...cleans out the throat and the mind. Scream. Yell at me. I am listening."

"I refuse. You should have told me that Willow was setting me up."

"It was for her to say." He shrugged and admired the way Jessica's hair flowed back and away from her face as she stalked toward him. Her gown was slit to the thigh, flowing around her body, pronouncing her breasts, the sway of her hips, defining that V between her legs. His body was hard now, needing to feel hers taut and hungry, and yet soft and hot against his. He steeled himself against reaching for her, from sealing her lips with his own.

"I don't like being manipulated and if Willow weren't such a good friend, I would really be angry. She thinks I'm over-worked and need a rest, and she thinks that here is a good place to do that."

"It is." But despite his bruised pride, Alexi remembered Howard and how he had looked at Jessica, the harm he could do to her. Alexi had to keep her close and know that she was safe. Because of that, he told himself, he served her a challenge. "I'm surprised you're still here. I didn't think that you would lower yourself by staying here—in this house with me... It's not exactly the luxury suite at the Amoteh. You might have to work once in a while. I mean physical work, not just calling your secretary—"

She scowled up at him. "You think I don't work? That I don't work every day? That I can't do physical labor? Listen, Mr. Stepanov—I fought my way through every inch of my life. I do so know how to work."

"You're raising your voice, Mrs. Sterling. I'm only saying that I need help here, and if you think I could work for a business you owned, then maybe you might want to work for me. But then, I can't see you doing that—settling into small-town life, helping me, letting the world know that uptown Jessica Sterling—"

"I run a corporation. There are obligations, major ones. You're asking a lot, Alexi." She was almost sizzling now; Alexi could feel the waves of heat and temper flowing from her.

"So do you." He was gambling now, desperate to keep her with him, to protect her, but to nourish what could be between them. "I want to see you every day, not just when you have time to drop by for a quickie—"

"That sounds awful."

"It sounds like a busy lady with a hunger. I'd appreciate the need—it's a compliment any man would like—but I'm not going to be your delivery boy. And you are not setting me up in business.''

Jessica breathed deeply and Alexi couldn't resist looking down at the cleavage revealed by her gown. He forced his eyes to slowly rise to Jessica's shadowed green ones. ''Yes, I want you. But more of you than just your body, or emotional pieces of you. Stay. Trust me.''

''Or? Or could it be that you don't trust me?'' she asked, moving closer to stand in front of him, looking up at him. She leaned slightly forward, her breasts soft and distinct against him. ''You don't, do you, Alexi? You're uncertain and it shows. You're pushing for a commitment. It's early for that, isn't it?''

''No,'' he stated flatly. ''It isn't. I think you'll run from this—what we have. Maybe it's too real for you, Mrs. Sterling.'' He wanted her, of course. But more than that, he wanted Jessica where he could protect her—because he was certain that Howard wasn't finished, that he couldn't let Jessica go, especially to a ''down-and-out cowboy.''

And maybe Howard would be right in one aspect of his thinking. Jessica was definitely a woman worth fighting for, even if it was fighting what ran uneasy within her.

Alexi wound a silky strand around his finger and tugged slightly. ''You can't take it. With an unfinished house, the temper you have will be crawling out. We're not sweethearts, either one of us, and things could get tense. Because I am an experienced builder and I suspect you are not, I would be directing you—your boss, so to speak—telling you what to do, and you wouldn't like that, would you? Why, you might actually yell, Mrs. Sterling.''

She lifted her fingertip and drew a nail down his shoulder. The gesture was feminine and taunting. ''What are you after, Stepanov?''

''You,'' he said simply, and swept her up in his arms. He carried her to his bed and dumped her upon it, enjoying the wild spread of her hair, the gown molding her body, a contrast to her pale skin. Lying on his side facing her, Alexi ran his hand along the smooth curve of her leg and trailed his fingertip upward, across her lower belly and down her other thigh. He enjoyed the quickening heat beneath his touch, the slow hiss of her indrawn breath, a sign that she reacted instantly to him— as he did to her. "You'll leave. You won't be able to—"

Her hand reached out to grip his jeans' waistband and she tugged slightly. "You're in for a surprise, buddy. Come here."

"Is it a surprise I'm going to like?" he teased against her lips.

"Just try to keep up, will you?"

Eight

"**Y**ou just couldn't wait for a report, could you, Willow?" Jessica asked as she turned off her laptop. Because she felt so incredibly light and happy, she couldn't stop smiling. She rose from the makeshift desk, a door placed across two sawhorses, and walked to Willow.

Seated on the floor in Alexi's house and warmed by the stove, Willow had been examining the seashells she'd collected from the beach. She grinned up at Jessica. "Less than one week—yes, I stayed away this long because I thought you'd get all worked up again about my little playacting.... You're blooming, you know. All lit up. All that tension is gone from your expression, that tight, overworked look. You look like you could fly, if you wanted. I'm so glad you're here."

"I am, too." Jessica bent to hug Willow and to kiss her cheek. She'd learned that from Robert and her friend—that showing emotion, especially love, wasn't something to hide for fear of it being used against her. She kissed Willow's cheek again and playfully wiggled her fingers on top of her head, diving through that mass of curls to the scalp below. "I'm happy. Really happy. It's only temporary. I don't think it can last, but Alexi is— I like him. I really do. He'll move on to someone permanent, and they'll be married and have the family all these Stepanovs love. I'll be glad for him."

"Dream on. And I don't think that's going to happen. Not if you give him a chance."

Jessica smiled and studied the shell Willow had just handed her. "Pretty. What you're saying is also very pretty, not reality. I know you have great hopes for Alexi and I. I just discovered the great deception a week ago—how you got me here, involved with Alexi. Yes, I'm staying here for a bit. But it's an extended holiday—my first real vacation in years—maybe a month or two of living high on fresh air and less stress. One of Robert's dear friends is taking over the bulk of my duties. I can do the rest from here."

Jessica was terrified. She didn't fit into this community, the warmth of the Stepanov family, and Alexi was definitely a family man. *What was she doing?*

"His family is coming over this morning to have coffee. We've been at their houses, and I thought… I don't know why I did, but I just invited them over to see what he's done—the men have been here, but I thought— Oh, Willow. I've arranged conferences and board meetings for years, and now I'm scared that I won't know how to make this wonderful family comfortable." Jessica looked around the neat living quarters. "I couldn't do much, but I did straighten up. Jarek and Alexi brought in that lovely big walnut hutch for some of his mother's things. I put the sweet rolls from the bakery and bottles of juice on it, and I've made coffee on the stove, but— I want this to be nice. Is it? I mean, it's just basic, but is it okay?"

"It's perfect and so are you. Told you. You really do need this, Jessica, to get away for a bit. You've been on thin ice for the last year or so. You know, if I get into the candle-making business heavily, I could probably hire area kids to collect these. But then, that would leave me with all the work and not the fun."

"So don't get any big ideas about being a maid of honor at

my wedding. This is only temporary. Alexi doesn't think I can manage life in a small town, or working for my keep—as if that's not what I've been doing. I'm going to show Alexi that I can handle whatever he throws at me. And I—I rather like the thought of rebuilding this house into something for his father. If he's anything like Fadey, he's adorable.'' Jessica took a long look at the makeshift desk, the heavy door spread over sawhorses, and mourned the work ahead of her. Had she really been working fourteen-hour days? Was it possible she'd handled this much work and hadn't taken time to relax, even on weekends?

James Thomas, one of Robert's friends and a stockholder in the company, welcomed the chance to give her a much-needed vacation. Aided by e-mail and overnight mail and the fax facility of her laptop, she could continue to work part-time on the empire Robert had loved so much.

''Delegate duty,'' Robert had warned her. ''Keep yourself intact and strong by taking time off and relaxing. I don't want you to kill yourself over this, Jessica. You're a young woman and I'm only enjoying the time we have together. I love you, Jess. Thank you for giving me so much. I would never have lived this long without you. Howard will want control. Do what is easiest for you, dear. Turn to James when you need help and support. He's been my lifelong friend. I am leaving my shares to you, not my son who already has a fair amount.''

Jessica listened to Alexi's and Jarek's heavy work boots tromping across the roof. Their voices carried downstairs in a deep rumble that somehow comforted her. She should have already returned to her Seattle offices, but the tilt of Alexi's head and the narrowing glint of his eyes had challenged her. Adept to doing business while traveling, Jessica had said, ''I'll need a couple days before I can start helping you full-time.''

He'd crossed his arms and his head went back, those ice-blue eyes glittering down at her. ''Okay. You're leaving for the office in Seattle.''

''No, I'm staying here. I've got most of what I need to start in my briefcase. My secretary can ship the rest. It's a big business, Alexi. One of Robert's friends is temporarily stepping in, but I'll have to continue working at times. Can you rig me a desk?''

She'd enjoyed his quick frown, that stunned look. Then Alexi had walked to a heavily varnished and restored old door. ''Good enough?''

When she'd nodded, Alexi had added, ''Tell Audrey to send pie and that I love her. She and her family are welcome here at any time. My family will make them comfortable until this place is better.''

He'd walked to her and gathered her close. ''Good,'' he whispered simply against her temple. ''This is good.''

Jessica followed the heavy clomping of footsteps across the roof. Had she really missed so much of life? In one week with Alexi, she knew and understood more texture about life than she'd learned in a lifetime. ''He wants me to yell, Willow. I've never done that in my life, but he's pushing his luck.''

''Huh?'' Willow asked, her eyes raised to the old ceiling tile stained with moisture. She traced the progression of men across the roof. ''I've always thought you should yell. Just to relieve pressure. It's good therapy.''

''Does it resolve the problem? Does it get this mountain of work done? Can you see tangible results?'' Jessica asked, though her mind was on the stack of papers that had been faxed to her and a new one scrolling out on her tiny portable printer.

Willow grinned and said, ''Oh, you'll yell. I'd bet on it. Alexi isn't the kind of man to let you bar him out of your life.''

''You know so much, do you? What's the bet?''

''That you'll take over my delivery and shuttle duties for the elderly here. I love them so much. But Mom is arranging a family get-together in Oregon. I want to go, but I can't leave them stranded here needing their groceries and appointments.''

''I'd do that anyway—without the bet, Willow.'' Jessica turned to the rough wood panel on the ceiling that was being pulled aside. A workman's boot and then, in a flurry of saw-dust, Alexi's jeans-clad legs appeared at the wooden ladder as he came down into the main room.

''Nice butt,'' Willow murmured with a grin. ''Two nice

butts, tight and hard,'' she corrected as Jarek made his way down. Intent upon a discussion of proper roofing trusses and supports, the men continued to talk.

''To get enough pitch for that overhang on the deck, we'll have to raise the roof.'' Alexi said to Jarek, and drew the carpenter's pencil from over his ear. He began marking on a fresh board propped against the wall.

Jarek pointed to the drawing. ''Raise it only on one side. Run a row of windows beneath the high side, down to the lower one.''

As if Alexi sensed where Jessica was standing, he turned to her and instantly the air between them started to vibrate and sizzle. She could feel him moving over her, in her. She could taste his skin, his mouth, feel his hair slide across her stomach. A week of long, sweet, exhausting nights had only increased their hunger. Jessica had thought that heat and hunger would be eased, but instead it had simmered through the days and ignited at one touch, one look. Yesterday, while having tea at Fadey and Mary Jo's, Alexi had looked at her with that dark intimate passion, and she'd heated immediately. Embarrassed by her need, her hands had trembled on the ornate metal holder for the glass, until Alexi had taken it from her. ''We're going,'' he'd said abruptly.

His excuse that they wanted to work on Viktor's house was barely believable, and they'd arrived, breathless with hunger, tumbling into bed....

Now Alexi's darkened gaze swept possessively down Jessica's body and then back up to lock with her eyes. He was still nettled that she had talked to Barney, but they hadn't discussed it again.

There was something else disturbing Alexi. He tensed every time a car went by, when one of their cell phones rang—and he was never far away, or if he was, one of his relatives always appeared.

The two men continued talking as they walked out of the door into the enclosed outer room. The door closed, a power saw buzzed and Jessica sighed. At times she had gone to stand outside the building to make business calls on her cell phone.

"Make a list of who needs what, Willow. I'll see that everyone gets delivered and picked up."

It wouldn't—couldn't—last, not that incredible passion, the quiet peace later lying close to Alexi....

Lost in her thoughts, Jessica frowned. She'd already given away too much of herself to Alexi, something she'd never given anyone else—including Robert. "What was that you were saying about Alexi?"

"I said, if you help Alexi, work part-time on the business and run a shuttle service, you're going to be really tired."

"I've been tired before. You do it, Willow, run a business and run errands. I run a corporation. That's not easy, you know. Everything, business and life, can be scheduled."

Willow smirked impishly. "Oh, really. Alexi can be scheduled? Does your schedule allow for extracurricular Alexi-activities?"

Then she frowned slightly and went to place her hand on Jessica's arm. "Did you tell him that Howard has been threatening you?"

"Howard is just hot air. He'll cool down. He has before."

"If you say so, Jessica. I know how you feel about doing your best for him, about your promise to his father. But this is different—"

"Did Alexi say anything?"

Willow looked away, avoiding the question, and Jessica pressed, "Did Alexi say anything to you about Howard?"

Her friend shrugged. "Okay, we talked briefly outside this morning. I said you had handled Howard for seven years before you married Robert and after, and that you knew him well enough to protect yourself."

"And?"

"And Alexi said things might be different this time. And this time, you wouldn't be alone. I liked that. It's a chick thing, maybe, but I know you're safe with him. The Stepanov men are big on taking care of their own."

Jessica stared at Willow. "I'm not helpless, you know. I take care of myself. I always have."

"Uh-huh. Don't get your nose out of joint. I'm not saying

you're bad at taking care of yourself, but you've never had a relationship before. And Alexi is one heck of a starting package—a total package.'' Willow glanced at the door that had opened again as Ellie, heavy with child, entered the room. Tanya, bundled against the cold, leaned shyly against her. Leigh, slightly rounded in pregnancy and balancing Katerina on her hip, followed. ''Alexi said to come right in, that you were expecting us. Is that all right?''

From the sunroom, Mikhail ordered loudly, ''My wife needs to sit down.''

A moment later he peeked inside the door to see that Ellie had followed his orders. Satisfied to find her seated in a chair, he nodded and closed the door.

''Mr. Mother Hen, and I love him. I hope we're not intruding,'' Ellie said softly, and rubbed the small of her back.

Jarek came in carrying a box and Leigh pointed to the hutch. ''Put it there, Pops.''

He beamed at her and carefully placed the cardboard box on the hutch. He peered inside and Leigh said, ''Oh, no, you don't. Not yet. Go get the other box.''

Before he left, Jarek bowed deeply, gallantly. ''I live to serve, milady.''

''Please make yourself comfortable. I'd love the visit,'' Jessica said as panic rose to tighten her throat. *She'd never had any friends, except Robert and Willow! In her lifetime, she'd never hosted a comfortable informal friendly gathering!* ''All I can offer is coffee and tea. There are rolls from the bakery on the hutch. I'm afraid—''

''Good. Food. I need some now.'' On her way to the sweet rolls, Leigh handed Katerina to Jessica. The toddler's chubby body was warm and cuddly, and instantly the unexpected ache for her own child bloomed inside Jessica. The thought terrified her; she'd come from a background where children weren't prized and she hadn't dreamed of a child since she was that innocent teenage bride.

She watched Leigh place a plastic cake carrier on the table, then take paper plates and plastic forks from a sack. Bottles of juice followed. Then Jarek came in again carrying a bigger box to the table.

Ellie looked at Mikhail who had just carried in another box, framed in a wooden crate. "On the table, please, Mikie," she purred and batted her eyelashes, evidently teasing him.

He slanted a mock-stern frown her way and hurried to open the door. Jarek and Alexi were muscling in a new apartment-size electric stove, and the three men set to installing it in one side of the large room. The women seemed comfortable amid the masculine discussion of electric codes and wiring and position.

"Open the boxes, Jessica," Ellie said softly. "They were Alexi's mother's things. Viktor wanted you to be able to use them."

In a daze, Jessica moved to the table and slowly opened the big box. Paper rattled as she withdrew a perfect china cup splashed with colorful flowers and trimmed in gold. She lifted another wrapping and a beautiful matching saucer appeared. The china was obviously old and precious to this family and Jessica felt her throat begin to close with emotion.

"Louise and Viktor's *samovar* is in the other box," Ellie said quietly, her expression soft and understanding as tears came to Jessica's eyes. "It's nice, having your own set, having a family to enjoy it with you."

Touched by the warmth of this family, Jessica fought back tears. She hadn't realized how much richness her life had lacked, how brittle it now seemed.

Who was she really? How much had she missed? And finally, what if she failed?

She found Alexi staring at her, and turned away. She didn't suit him, or this family. What was she thinking, involving herself with Alexi, a man who had already been hurt?

What was she doing?

Alexi wiped his hands on the rag and stood, studying the newly installed kitchen sink and counter. His cousins and uncle were already enjoying sweet rolls and coffee in the next room and Alexi couldn't put off joining them any longer.

Jessica was clearly emotional and off-balance, uncomfortable amidst the sudden burst of Stepanovs. She'd seemed helpless and afraid, and yet she didn't turn to him, preferring to keep her fears to herself.

So he was angry and frustrated, and wanted to hold her. But her head had gone up with pride and once again she'd cut him from her life, from what caused her to react so emotionally, almost stunned by family warmth.

He threw down the rag and, unable to prolong it any longer, walked into the living area. Once there he stopped, caught by the image of Jessica sitting on the floor. Her legs were folded, the toddler seated upon them. Her hair was down, waving around her face, and she seemed softly, warmly, stunned as she spoke with his family. She seemed locked in a discovery that pleased and frightened her.

Then Jessica met his gaze and tears shimmered in her eyes. Her lips opened and trembled, as if she were trying to speak.

Alexi moved quickly to her. He gently picked up the toddler and handed her to Jarek, then he lifted Jessica into his arms. Alexi sat in the big rocking chair that had just been brought from the shop and held Jessica, rocking her gently while his family continued to talk softly.

"I can't do this," Jessica whispered.

"I know," he returned, challenging her. "It's too easy. You like the fight, don't you?"

"Rat."

When they were alone, Alexi watched Jessica carefully place the china cups and saucers onto a huge hutch. Her fingers ran over the gleaming, ornate *samovar* as if treasuring it.

He placed the new secretary desk he had just carried inside on the floor. Jarek had left it in the sunroom and Alexi preferred to give his gift to Jessica in private. "Where do you want this?"

"What?" As if reluctant to leave the Stepanov gifts, Jessica turned slowly. "It's beautiful, Alexi. But not necessary. You can take it back to the furniture display room, or the shop. The door will do nicely—"

She frowned and came closer. "I haven't seen this design before. It's beautiful, very feminine, almost sensual."

In comparison to the emerald rings she wore, glittering as her hand swept across the desk, the walnut secretary was nothing—and it was everything, a gift of his heart to the woman he suspected he loved. "I made it for you. It's my own design."

Jessica frowned, clearly startled, her hand going over her heart. "You made it. For me," she repeated.

Alexi swallowed the emotion in his throat. "I hope you like it. Now, where do you want it?"

"For me? Is that how you see me? Like the beauty in this?" she repeated once more, as if disbelieving. A tear dropped from her lashes and slid down her cheek. "No one has ever made me a gift before," she added shakily.

"It is only a small thing, something a man does for a woman he—cherishes," he finished unevenly. He placed the secretary on the floor and reached to cradle her face in his hand. His thumb stroked away the tear and he replaced it with a light kiss.

"It's lovely. I—I don't know what to say." Jessica felt as if all the brittle pieces of armor she'd pasted around her through the years were coming apart.

She didn't expect to see the pain in his face, or the tears. "Alexi, I am fine."

"You say you're always 'fine,' don't you?" His deep voice was rough with emotion. "But you show me what you feel, behind that smoke screen you use to protect yourself."

She couldn't stop the tears flowing down her cheeks. "Why are you so angry?"

"Because my gift is so little, so simple, a man to a woman, and it terrifies you. You should have had presents before…made with—" He stopped and turned from her. "I want to take you someplace. If you want to go, put on your boots and jacket. It's cold outside."

"No. Not now."

Alexi raised a dark brow. "You don't trust me, even for that?"

"I just want to stay here…where it's all so beautiful. I'm afraid if I leave, it will all disappear…."

His frown deepened. "This is a good house. It's rough now, but it's not going anywhere."

How could she explain? "No, I'm afraid all the warmth and love will—"

Alexi tugged her into his arms and his light kisses dried her tears. "You think too much."

"This is only temporary, you know. There's a real world out there, and it isn't going to wait. Just hold me tight, Alexi. I feel as if I'm coming apart."

His body stiffened, but he held her tightly against him. *Temporary* with Jessica wasn't a word he liked, yet it was better than nothing with her.

Layers of morning fog blurred the sight of Jessica walking along the beach in front of Alexi. Sandpipers zigzagged along the sand, picking at bits of food; seagulls cried like tiny white ghosts before settling upon piers circled by thick cables.

She had been unsettled throughout the night, walking out onto the deck to stare at the night, to listen to the crash of the waves. More than once, she had passed by the hutch holding his mother's old china, touching the pieces almost reverently. She'd sat at the desk he'd made, running her hands over the smooth, oiled wood, rearranging her laptop and pencils and pads several times.

Alexi rubbed his chest, where the ache had started inside his heart and watched Jessica.

She began to walk toward the deserted pier that the summer would fill with tourists, browsing in the shops and sitting in lawn chairs with bait and tackle boxes at their sides, fishing lines in the water.

This is only temporary, she'd said, and the words had hurt him desperately. They closed the door to the future they could have, that he wanted.

Alexi reached down to pick up a smooth flat stone and sent it skipping across the dark waves. And what did he have to offer her?

Was she thinking of her late husband, the man she had loved?

Was Alexi so fragile that he needed her to say the words to him, to come after him, initiate lovemaking desperately, to give him a sign that she cared? How much time did they have before she went back to Seattle, to the elegant home and wealth he couldn't give her?

Alexi watched her disappear into the fog lying over the tourists' pier. *How could he let her go?*

How long could he dance around saying what he wanted, pushing for a commitment that might terrify her?

Alexi inhaled roughly, holding the cold, salt-scented air inside him before releasing it. He knew himself. He wasn't a man to wait and he wasn't a man to avoid the inevitable confrontation with the bully hounding her. Jessica's independent nature wouldn't like his interference.

By the last week of January, just two weeks since Alexi and she had first made love, Jessica had dug into her new role, not exactly a peaceful change, but definitely more exciting. Not only was she discovering how much she liked everyday life in Amoteh, the Stepanov family, but she felt energized. She wasn't simply a mechanical body filling an office position. She wasn't drained by mountains of responsibilities and paperwork, and then returning the next day for the endless tasks.

Instead she had found that life in Amoteh settled her into a peace she'd never known. She enjoyed the good times the Stepanov women shared, the way Ellie had settled into a quiet anticipation of her baby, which was due the first week of February.

She had carefully filtered her cell phone calls, not answering Howard's. Because of business, she restricted him to e-mail contact, and he was angry. Too bad. The newly installed land line also had a Caller ID attached and Howard was simply ignored.

Jessica was in her own perfect bubble, complete with a man who made her feel—really feel like she was alive and thriving. In Alexi's arms, Jessica was all woman—and that held a beauty and power of its own, so deep and powerful that it glowed inside her.

Sometimes. There were times when she could shake him, as if that was possible.

Jessica stared at Alexi, who was above her repairing the roof. Through the makeshift hole, which would later become a skylight, he glared down at her. "I said, 'roofing nails.' This is a wood screw."

"Listen, bud. Be glad. You got me up at the crack of dawn and you haven't stopped pushing me since. I haven't done anything right all day—according to you. And you've gotten sawdust all over the floor. I just used the shop vacuum on it."

His smile wasn't nice. "That happens when wood is sawed. It makes sawdust."

"I've been up and down this ladder so much that my butt hurts."

"I need roofing nails, not wood screws, and a claw hammer isn't a crowbar."

"First, I wasn't holding my end of the replacement window high enough and you yelled at me."

"Yell back. Go back to your office work. But get me the nails first, I'm losing daylight."

Her temper rising, Jessica held back the shout almost ready to burst into the air between them. "You know I never yell," she said unsteadily. "I'll get your damn nails.... What did you just mutter?"

"Nothing."

"You just said 'women,' like that, like—" Jessica realized she had just shouted. "Now look what you've made me do."

Around the nail between his lips, Alexi said, "Sure. You yelled, and now you're blaming your bad temper on me."

He took the nail from his lips and began to hammer above her. Jessica wasn't done with him. "You shouldn't have started it, Stepanov."

"Get off that ladder. I'll get the nails myself. The right nails. Go bake some cookies or play with your computer. I'm losing daylight," he repeated.

"You're going to lose a lot more than that." Jessica backed

down the ladder, giving way to Alexi who was descending.
She stood to one side and crossed her arms. "Alexi, you are
an evil, temperamental, bullying, single-minded, arrogant—"

He walked to an assortment of sacks, selected one, filled the
pouch at his workman's belt and held up a nail in front of her.
"This is a roofing nail," he said, spacing out the words as if
speaking to a small child. "A screw has little ridges running
around it."

"Rat," Jessica finished her assessment of the man who had
nudged her temper all day.

She studied Alexi, who was dumping the old removed nails
into a can. Sawdust was in his hair and a little had caught in
the dark stubble on his chin. He was wearing a worn, quilted
plaid shirt against the cold, jeans that revealed his thermal un-
derwear through the torn places in them, and work boots that
had definitely seen better days.

"I am not going to the Seagull's Perch tonight while you
tend bar," she said unevenly to keep herself from shouting.
"I've had enough of you for the day. So far, I'm not intelligent
enough to hold a level steady or use a nail gun. And just by
the way, you've laid out the kitchen wrong. Add that to the
way you do not roll the toothpaste tube from the bottom and—
What are you looking at me like that for?"

"Are you going to yell again? It sounds like you're getting
worked up enough to—"

Jessica stepped close to Alexi and grabbed his shirt in her
fist. She stood on tiptoe to frown up at him. "I never yell,"
she said between her teeth. "Got it?"

"I think you are going to yell," Alexi stated quietly, watching her. "You did a while ago."

"No, I won't and no, I didn't."

"Okay," he said lightly, and lifted her hand to kiss her palm.
While her mind stopped and churned and tried to find steady
ground, Alexi bent to kiss her lightly, his tongue flicking lightly
across her parted lips. Then he picked her up by the waist and
lifted her aside; he walked into the living area and into the
kitchen.

Jessica followed quickly; Alexi could confuse her too easily.

"You can't just shift an argument from a heated discussion—"

Alexi frowned and studied the kitchen layout. He opened and shut the small temporary refrigerator's door. He turned the water faucet on and off. "You were getting worked up to yell. What's wrong with this layout?"

"I was discussing…repeat, discussing, how arrogant you are. You can't just kiss my hand and me in the middle of it. That changes the rules."

"We have rules? I thought we were just going with the flow, as Bliss and Ed say. The sink here, the refrigerator here, dishwasher here—pantry and laundry room combination just off the kitchen. There's nothing wrong with this design."

"We do have rules. One of them is that you can't talk to me like a child."

"You are no child," he said firmly. "But you are used to ordering people around and you are *my* assistant. I am not yours."

"Do women really put up with your arrogance?"

"Since I am *temporarily*—as you say—out of commission with any woman other than you, how would I know that? And I am not arrogant. I simply know what I am doing. How many remodeling jobs have you done? I've done a few and there is nothing wrong with this layout."

"I've designed traffic flows, aisle promotions, and so on. This 'assistant' knows that you've got the refrigerator clear at the other end of the kitchen. If the door is open, it will block anyone from coming into the kitchen from the living room. And the dishwasher should be close to the sink. You really should make the window longer and the sill wider for potted herbs."

Alexi frowned and rubbed his index finger up and down beneath his lips. "Hmm."

He crouched to scratch off the names of the appliances on the floor and scribbled new ones.

"Alexi, I do not like how you—"

He stood and looked down at her, then leaned back against

the counter. "What's the matter? Can't you keep up, Sterling?"

"You're determined to—"

He bent to kiss her again, this time nuzzling her cheek with his and whispering in her ear, "You're all rosy and warm, just like when you—"

This time Jessica grabbed his shirt with both fists. "You think you can get away with anything, don't you?"

"I like to think so," Alexi stated mildly, reaching to ease a strand of her hair behind her ear. He bent to nibble on her lobe. "What are you going to do about it?"

He hadn't shaved. His brilliant blue eyes were dancing with humor, the lines beside them crinkling, and there was that devastating grin, a boy at play tormenting a girl. To add to that image, Alexi reached out to tug one of the braids he'd fashioned for her earlier.

Alexi could be sweet, like when tugging her onto his lap to braid her hair. Or he could be tormenting, like now.

She could either retain her dignity, or she could— Jessica shoved her hands into his hair and tugged his head down for a kiss that she hoped would stun him. Then *she,* the champion in their tussles, would walk away…. Alexi was in for a big lesson at Jessica-school.

She had never come after him, but now nothing could stop her. She slanted her mouth on his, fusing the fit, then arched against him. Alexi's arms tightened around her, lifting her slightly until their stares met. "You're getting very physical and demanding, aren't you, Sterling?"

"Can't you keep up, Stepanov?" she asked huskily, and bent to gently nip the side of his throat, his earlobe. Hitching higher, she wrapped her legs around him. She watched Alexi, pleased that he'd seemed shocked at her play. She'd never played in sex before, teasing, demanding, taking that first initiative—

Alexi's hands cupped her bottom and, carrying her, he walked to their bed, turned and fell backward with her on top of him.

He lay quietly beneath her, watching, waiting.

"It's daylight," she said, weighing the hours until dark against her need for Alexi.

"We're losing it," he reminded her.

Jessica sat up astride him. She tugged off her overlarge sweat jacket, the overlarge sweater, all battered and worn, courtesy of Alexi's limited clothing. She began to unbutton his large flannel shirt and his eyes darkened into silver slits as she peeled it away, revealing her sports bra.

He was already aroused, layers of fabric separating them, and yet he hadn't touched her. The tiny lines around his tightly pressed lips said he was fighting the sensual taunt. There was nothing more challenging that a sensual battle with Alexi—it served to stoke her own hunger. The incredible freedom to expose her needs to Alexi, to know that she could control the pace, that he would always wait for her fullest pleasure, astounded her.

Jessica slowly slipped out of her sports bra and tossed it aside. She smiled at Alexi and rode that slight movement of his rising hips. "Oh, oh, got to go," she said, and put one leg out, her toes reaching for the floor.

She loved this game—hunting, chasing, teasing Alexi, because she knew it would always end the same. She laughed as Alexi reacted instantly, tugging on her wrist. He toppled her gently in the opposite direction, flat on the bed, and pinned her with his body. "You think so, do you?"

His hand ran down to the bow in her sweatpants, tugging it free and easing away the pants and the thermalwear beneath it. Cupping her briefly, Alexi ran his fingers along the elastic of her briefs and stroking her gently, found the liquid, intimate warmth. Jessica caught her breath, the cords of her body tightening, her skin heating, that melting hunger that needed feeding. Her fingers dug into his shoulders as she forced herself to breathe quietly. She could already feel the riveting storm, feel herself traveling into the tight, passionate tunnel, spiraling upward—

With a grin he said, "Oh, oh, got to go," repeating her tease.

"Oh, no, you don't," she said as her own hands began to work, her body already undulating to the heavy pressure of his.

In a flurry of hands and open mouths and hunger, Alexi was soon undressed. He let her turn him easily, his hands cupping her breasts as she rose over him, already accepting his fullness, bending to the pleasure of his kiss, tasting the heat and hunger rise desperately, feverishly in him.

One tug of his mouth's suction and Jessica let go the quiet scream of pleasure, her body already tightening, bunching for a release.

But Alexi wanted more, demanded more, making her wait until their bodies were slick with sweat, every heartbeat racing. Suddenly, Jessica could no longer wait, freeing the pleasure, letting it burst within her, through her.

Later she lay within Alexi's arms, her body tangled with his, her cheek against his shoulder. He stroked her back, nuzzled her head, and as his heart slowed its race, he kissed her damp forehead.

Whatever had been bothering him loomed, almost palpable between them.

Then Alexi was untangling their bodies, rising from the bed, almost as if he couldn't bear to touch her....

Naked, broad shoulders gleamed in the dim light outlining his body as Alexi slid into his jeans and walked into the kitchen.

Puzzled at his change of mood from playful to sensual and then to brooding, Jessica slowly drew on his flannel shirt and followed.

She found Alexi, his hands braced on the counter, looking out at the thin line of brilliant orange separating the night sky from the black waves. ''Alexi? What's wrong?''

Nine

She wore another man's ring.

Jessica considered what they had to be "temporary."

And Alexi wanted everything!

Alexi stiffened as Jessica's open hand smoothed his back and she asked again, "Alexi?"

He turned to her abruptly. Alexi considered Jessica's vulnerable, concerned expression, her cheeks flushed by their love-making, her lips swollen from his kiss. She looked like a child, mussed from sleep, in his overlarge flannel shirt—until he noted her long, smooth legs, legs that had wrapped around him, her body gloving his, making them one.

She hid so much of herself from him—those tight little inner emotions. When she touched his mother's china, it was with reverence and fear of breaking the pieces. But it was more than that, as if she were storing memories to last long after she'd left him.

What would Jessica do if she knew how deeply he already loved her? That each time they made love, he thought about his own child growing within her?

Uncertain in his frustration, Alexi rapped at her. "You bought a new shuttle bus, complete with handicap facilities. You bought wheelchairs and other medical necessities for those who needed them. You donated to the clinic."

She frowned, her hand upon his chest now, smoothing the area over his aching heart. "Yes, I did. Willow has a new van, and I needed the shuttle so that I could carry more people on outings. Corporations donate for tax deductions. It serves everyone."

He caught her wrist, capturing it just as he wanted to do with the woman, to keep her by his side. To make his life with her. "Does that mean you're staying? You live here, work with me every day, and when I'm tending bar, you're at your desk, working."

"I don't see the problem, Alexi."

"You wouldn't. You're on an extended vacation, right? What if I want more than this month? Or six months. Or forever. What then?"

His gut tightened painfully as Jessica paled and her hand moved away; another man's emeralds glittered in the dim light. The demand that he'd pushed back too often surged roughly to his lips. "What am I to you?"

Alexi could barely breathe; her answer was too long in coming, too thoughtful.

"Well, you're definitely not my fun-time guy—except when you want to be. You can be charming, boyish and most of all unpredictable. Top that off with bossy, arrogant, swaggering, macho, brooding, whatever, and I guess that would be you. I doubt that anyone knows just exactly what a pain in the butt you can be, Stepanov."

"You know what I mean." He ran his hand through his hair. Jessica let him into her life just that bit, and then the doors slammed shut.

"This is all so beautiful," Jessica whispered unevenly. "I'm discovering all sorts of things about myself, Alexi. It's terrifying to discover that I want a man so badly that I'd forget where my obligations lie…that I am tempted to drop a promise to a man who helped me survive."

Alexi frowned and crossed his arms. Unlike the lover of a short time ago, he seemed formidable, foreign and dangerously on edge. "Your obligations are to yourself, to what you feel."

"No, you don't understand what Robert did for me. On his deathbed, he asked me to see to Howard, to help him. I said I would. I—Robert was the father I never had. He was my mentor and my friend—"

"I know." He'd been wrong to push her, and seeing her torn between her obligation and what Alexi wanted hurt him, as well. Putting aside his needs, Alexi reached to gather her into his arms. He picked her up and carried her to the big rocking chair, easing to sit with her. Jessica reached to take the soft throw from the back and spread it over them, covering his bare shoulder with the cloth on one side; on the other, she rested her head. She sighed unevenly, dabbed the cloth at her damp eyes and settled against him. "I could stay like this forever."

The wooden chair began to creak as Alexi rocked her. For the moment he gave himself to the peace of having Jessica in his arms. But he knew he would want more than "temporary." "That's your decision."

While Alexi was out at the Seagull's Perch remodeling the storage room, Jessica lay on the house's floor, next to Tanya, gardening books spread open in front of them. The mid-March winds howled around the corners of the house, snug now with the renovations. Baby Sasha was in her Moses cradle, sleeping until her next feeding—a bottle of her mother's breast milk. Meanwhile, Ellie and Mikhail were enjoying a romantic dinner at the Amoteh.

According to Viktor, mid-March was the perfect time to plant potatoes and they had, just today. The huge garden space had been plowed and tilled, waiting for vegetable seeds. Jessica had known how to cut "seed" potatoes, keeping an "eye" in each section and letting them dry somewhat before planting.

She'd missed the simple rhythm of life that she'd known as a child, the planting of a garden and watching it grow. She missed hanging sheets on a sunlit clothesline, and the new one that Alexi had built was perfect. So perfect that she'd stood between the lines of sheets, crying so that he couldn't see her.

Discovering her there, he'd seemed so angry—his thumb testing the dampness on her cheek. And then Alexi had tugged her into his arms, holding her tight and safe where she could hear the comforting beat of his heart.

"Temporary" was a big word. Maybe he felt, as she did, that this beautiful time together was only a slice in time.

She had made two brief necessary visits to her office in Seattle, and Alexi had insisted going with her. Of course, he'd concealed his purpose to protect her against Howard with the need to secure various hardware—any of which could have been ordered through catalogs or online. In her house, Alexi— a man raised on a Western ranch and used to big expanses of sky, water and land—was restless and uncomfortable. While watching him put aside his needs to see to her safety, Jessica knew that her home was back in Amoteh, in the cozy house they were remodeling together—in the gleaming floors, the big, wide Stepanov bed....

Tanya brought Jessica back to the present; the girl's small finger traced a picture of pansies. "Pansies are happy, aren't they? Like little faces? Viktor said his wife liked pansies, especially deep purple ones. Grandpa Fadey says that we are going to grow lots of raspberries and that I can pick them and that Grandma Mary Jo says that I can help her make his favorite-ever cookies."

The cycle of life was here in Amoteh, changing seasons with the Stepanov family, with Alexi....

Years ago, Jessica had left a dirt-poor farm, a family who didn't care—and she was never going back. What would Alexi think of a woman who couldn't bear to see her parents again? Who could never go home? She didn't want to give him the ugly pictures of that life, so different from this one.

Baby Sasha stirred and mewed lightly, and Jessica rose to change her diaper. Tanya began cutting pictures out of the catalogs to paste onto paper for Viktor.

Cradling the baby against her, smelling that sweet scent, Jessica heard the doorbell. Tanya, eager to show her parents her handiwork, sprang up to follow Jessica to the sunroom.

It would be beautiful, Jessica thought as she passed through the spacious room, the cool, practical, pebbled linoleum perfect to counterbalance potted herbs and seedlings, not ready for full sun. With the baby in her arms and Tanya at her side, Jessica opened the door.

On the back deck, the tall, cool blonde with artfully tossed long hair slowly took in Jessica's hair; it was twisted and lightly secured by a gigantic clip on top of her head. The blonde's cool, dark brown eyes roamed down Jessica's sweater, stained a little by the baby's last feeding. The picture-perfect woman, dressed in an expensive sweater and designer jeans and high-heeled boots, took in Jessica's paint-stained bib overalls and the hole in her left sock.

"Is Alexi here?" the woman asked in a low, husky tone. "I was told he lived here."

"He's at work—"

The woman's look was disdainful as she looked at the baby and down to wide-eyed Tanya who was clinging onto Jessica's leg. "The girl definitely isn't Alexi's. She's too old and he was quite busy over three years ago. Are these yours? Are you his—housekeeper? *Is the baby Alexi's?*"

Jessica adjusted the infant's flannel blanket around her head. However, Jessica could not adjust her rising temper, and perhaps jealousy, as easily. "It's too cold at the doorway for the baby. You'll find Alexi at the Seagull's Perch."

"I heard he bought it," the woman pressed. Behind the carefully emphasized and beautiful eyes, a female shark stirred, ready to bite. "His cousin, Mikhail Stepanov, said I'd find him here. Are you certain he isn't here? I'm Heather Pell. You may have seen my pictures in magazines—if you read them—or the society pages. We used to be engaged. I married someone else, but now I'm divorced. We—Alexi and I—were very close."

And we will be again, so make plans to be ousted, baby, was the underlying statement.

Mikhail always knew what he was doing: it was likely that he sent Heather to the house so she could see Alexi was involved with another woman. Jessica didn't appreciate the favor, not when she was dressed for remodeling and painting.

"No, these aren't his children and I haven't seen your picture—anywhere. He's at the tavern. Thank you for that information. Goodbye." Jessica closed the door and stood still, stunned by the woman's sudden appearance.

"Gosh, she's beautiful," Tanya said admiringly. Then she sneezed. "She smells yuck."

"Yes, she is pretty and that 'smell' is probably one-thousand-dollars-a-half-ounce of Parisian perfume." On her way to feed the baby, Jessica saw herself in the mirror—mussed hair, a shiny, clean face; she wore paint-stained bib overalls and eau d'enfant. Only months ago she had looked like a tired, brittle businesswoman trying to conceal the drain on her energy and pushing for more...

Heather Pell was an exciting, gorgeous femme fatale on the hunt. Would Alexi still find her attractive? Of course he would. What man wouldn't drool at the woman's sexual power, those long legs, that mass of blond hair?

Heather had hurt Alexi badly. After three years, he was still angry—still moody when Jessica and he had met. Back then, she'd experienced firsthand his bitterness and resentment for women who looked somewhat like Heather.

Jessica couldn't let that happen to him again. Jessica had protected a corporation for years. Now she decided to save her lover from a woman who devoured men and cast them aside for a bigger catch.

Her breath caught with the next thought: she'd never been jealous before and she'd just gotten a big, wide, red blast of that unsettling emotion. All because of Alexi.

At closing time Alexi glanced at the woman who had just entered the tavern. He did a double take and knew he was in trouble. Jessica wore that slinky female expression that shielded a determined angry one—if he was reading correctly those narrowed green eyes emphasized by mascara and the glossy set of her lips.

When a man's intended came strolling in to find another

woman all but spreading herself on the bar in front of him—
he was in deep, dangerous water.

Just divorced, Heather had come hunting him for an obvious
reunion—she wore the platinum engagement ring that had cost
Alexi a small fortune. And she wasn't taking no for an answer.
"I'm free now. It was all a mistake and I'm so sorry. We can
pick right up where we left off—"

Jessica placed the Amoteh Resort's wine and dinner basket
on a table with a thud and took off her coat. She wore a formfitting, long-sleeved gray sweater and tight black jeans. She
gripped the basket and, in her red high heels, walked slowly
toward him.

*Jessica was dressed to do business of a feminine kind and
he wasn't certain just how this scenario would end.*

Across the polished bar from Alexi, Heather wore a slinky,
slip-like lacy beige dress that showed her cleavage. She didn't
turn as Jessica walked slowly toward the bar; Alexi had moved
behind it, putting distance between Heather's clinging body and
his own.

The click of Jessica's heels against the floor sounded ominous.

Alexi breathed quietly; either Jessica would believe that he
hadn't touched Heather or she wouldn't. His pride kept him
from saying the same.

"Alexi…Heather," Jessica said, and Alexi felt the chill rise
up his nape.

"Heather was just leaving," he stated quickly, moving in to
defend himself.

Jessica's smile didn't go to her eyes. "Your cousin, Mikhail,
informed Heather that you might be at home. She came to visit
you there. Too bad you were here and she had to walk all the
way back to her car and then drive here."

Alexi groaned silently. Jessica was just getting warmed up.
Mikhail would have to pay for sending Heather to the house
and not to Alexi first. Jessica might never have known that his
ex-fiancée had visited—and exited his life forever.

Heather flashed the diamond ring in front of Jessica. "How
does it feel to come in second best?"

"You mean, Alexi?"

"Whatever."

Alexi inhaled sharply, uncertain of Jessica in this dangerous mood—but he knew that he had to head off trouble between the women. Heather knew how to ruin lives; she knew how to invent situations and tell lies.

Jessica glanced at Alexi and ordered pleasantly, "Stay out of this. I'll let you know if I need any help."

The tough businesswoman was back and, despite the signs of danger, Alexi had to admire Jessica. He swept out a have-at-it hand, and she nodded.

"You need your butt kicked, Heather," Jessica said too pleasantly. "You hurt Alexi badly."

Heather's smile didn't reach those cold, sharklike eyes. "You don't have what it takes to keep a man like Alexi satisfied, little miss housewife."

"Heather, watch it," Alexi warned. He was too familiar with Jessica's green eyes narrowing, with the temper behind them.

"You stay out of this."

Jessica spread her hands wide on the smoothly polished bar and looked at them. Then her eyes met Alexi's before moving to lock with Heather's. "Here's how I see it. You're starting to wear around the edges a bit, those little fine lines that a model can't afford. Or a status wife who gets replaced with a newer model. You probably made a killing on the divorce. But it's a hard, cruel world out there and now you want someone to take care of you—Alexi is good at that, isn't he? Taking care of a woman, making her feel safe? Supporting her when she's feeling down and out?"

"I need him," Heather admitted unevenly, with a ring of truth. A woman desperate for help and admitting defeat, Heather's eyes pleaded with Jessica. "I'm not used to handling my own—I lost most of what I got in the divorce. There's a monthly allowance—but Alexi always knew what to do when I needed him. I need him to tell me what to do now."

Though Heather's unexpected truths startled Alexi, Jessica didn't miss a beat. "You've got a lot of resources you haven't tapped. And you're ready to get out there on your own—without following a man's orders. Listen, I've been remodeling the house with Alexi and I can tell you, he isn't always right. Not a clue sometimes. You know how to relate to the camera, Heather. You could teach that skill to other models or speakers doing television spots. There's a whole thing about clothing and makeup when doing interviews, isn't there? You could run your own company.''

Heather's understandable fear of unwanted wrinkles quickly cleared her frown. ''You're right. Alexi doesn't have a clue sometimes. Neither do the other men I've depended on. Sure, I'm pretty and smart, but no one sees just how intelligent I am. Gorgeous can't last forever, you know. My class and brains will go a long way. I know a photographer who is always grousing about the models not relating to the camera, about not being able to open up. I was like that. I had a friend hold a camera on me night and day and I studied angles and got more comfortable—''

''See? It took brains to think of something like that.'' Jessica leveled a don't-interfere look at Alexi who was frowning at the ''he isn't always right'' and ''not a clue'' comments.

This time when Heather's eyes lit, it wasn't with anger. It was with hope. ''I think I just might be able to pull off some sort of tutoring or school. Alexi, you should have told me that sooner.''

''He probably had his mind on other things, like setting up a house for you, the marriage picture and babies and all that.'' Jessica shrugged and Alexi caught her ''I'm winning this one'' smirk before she said, ''You know how men are.''

''Yeah. Right. Men,'' Heather said as she tugged on her coat. ''They're always thinking of themselves. I'm out of here. I'm selling the ring, Alexi.''

Stunned at the unexpected sisterly interaction of the women, Alexi gave his go-for-it hand gesture; locked on her dream, Heather hurried out of the tavern. He studied Jessica, who was leaning back on the bar, braced by her elbows. He tugged her hair lightly. ''I love it when you smirk.''

''Uh-huh. You were desperate. You should have seen your

face when I walked in. A real picture of a guilty man caught in the act.''

"I was trying to get rid of her. She wasn't buying, and Heather can be real trouble when she's mad—she flies right past reason and dives into revenge. There are people around here that I don't want hurt. Shanghaiing a male troublemaker like Lars Anders is a bit different from a woman who can cry all sorts of things.... So you were protecting me. Fighting for my honor?''

"Something like that. Mikhail and Ellie picked up the children and he left this—I just thought you might want to share...or something.'' Jessica pushed free of the bar and, with slow, swaying hips, walked to the door. She locked it securely, flipped the Closed sign and picked up the Amoteh's wine and food basket. She walked to the stairs leading up to the tavern's second floor.

"Tell me you're not jealous,'' he said, testing her, enjoying pushing her just that bit to cause her to ignite—because she did so beautifully.

Jessica stopped and ordered huskily, "You owe me, Alexi. Pay up.''

This time, the knowing smirk was his as he followed her swaying hips up the stairs.

"You just yelled,'' Alexi said briskly as they stood in the kitchen. "All I said was to hold the head of the ceiling fan steady while I adjusted the supports for it in the attic.''

"And I said I was doing just that. I had to yell. You were in the attic at the time and you'd just yelled down at me. How could you hear me over your yelling, if I didn't yell?'' Jessica forced the words down to a too-quiet tone. "You are the most irritating person on the earth. I do not know why—yes, I do. I am determined not to let you get the best of me.... Do you hear me, Alexi?''

Concentrating on his work, Alexi took one of the fan's paddles from the box and rose on the step stool to attach it to the installed motorized head. "Hand me another.''

Jessica grabbed one and slapped it into his waiting hand.

"Back to what we were talking about before you escaped up the ladder to the attic. I get the feeling that every time you do not want to discuss money, you find someplace to hide, like in the crawl space working on plumbing. If you want the tavern, there is no reason why you can't borrow money from me— temporarily. You're just being stubborn. Or if not me, then borrow from one of your family."

He held out his hand for another paddle. "You just don't give up, do you? Go turn on the electricity—the right switch this time."

She didn't like the reminder that she had almost killed her lover. When Jessica came back into the room, she was prepared to argue her case. "It's mid-March, Alexi. Only a few days ago your friend, Miss Pell, came to see you. Tourist season is coming, and if you had ownership now, you could make those changes you wanted, like making that upper room suitable for an apartment."

He watched the fan's blades circle slowly, then stepped up on the ladder again. "Hand me the lightbulbs. I've changed my mind. I don't want to live in that apartment."

"But the view is gorgeous. The sunsets over the ocean—"

"It is. Perfect for an office. I don't want a home office— work interfering with life."

"I'm managing both right now. Multitasking is a part of business, Alexi."

"But you're temporary, aren't you? You're taking an 'extended vacation,' aren't you?" Alexi screwed in the lightbulb she handed him. "I made a down payment to Barney last week. He's going to stay on until this house is livable. Open the box that Fadey brought this morning. It's for you."

Jessica studied the slowly rotating blades, her thoughts circling her, as well. She loved every inch of the old house that had seemed to come to life. With the help of the Stepanovs, Alexi and she had almost finished the construction basics in the house. Every job, from drywall to painting and finishing the oak baseboards, had been an exciting adventure—and they'd made love on the new flooring, in the new bedroom—

in that big sturdy Stepanov bed—and in the sleeping bag out on the deck....

She couldn't put off life forever, and Howard's frustration and anger was rising. James Thomas's daily communications omitted Howard—which probably meant that a critical situation was brewing. She would have to eventually deal with Howard. To give the necessary appearance of a return to business, she'd made known her tentative plans to return to the office at the end of March—only two weeks away.

Each day was sweeter and more frightening.

Alexi wasn't the kind of man to let another threaten her; he would take action and that could endanger him. She had to protect Alexi and Sterling Stops, yet keep Howard pacified.

How could she ever leave this beautiful old house, even for a short time? She'd grown to love it so, and the whole Stepanov family, and the babies, Katerina and month-and-a-half-old Sasha. Then there was Mary Jo—almost a mother—the sisterhood of the younger women.... They'd wrapped her in a blanket of love, until she'd almost forgotten the harsh realities of her life.

Was she so wrong to leave her own family years ago, to make a life for herself away from the grasping tentacles that could destroy her?

Distracted by the decisions she needed to make, Jessica pulled her gaze away from the almost-hypnotic movement of the fan's blades.

She found Alexi's startling blue eyes watching her.

"Where were you just now?" he asked quietly as he smoothed a strand of hair from her cheek back into the bandanna covering her head.

The decisions she had to make were hers alone. She couldn't involve Alexi. "That fan style doesn't suit the clean, modern lines of the kitchen."

She looked at an unopened box sitting in the living space. 'I can't open that box. It's from your father, mailed to Fadey. Why didn't you tell me about the tavern? And I don't think I like that ceiling fan's style in this room. We should put this one in the bedroom and get one that doesn't have bulbs for the kitchen. *What?* You made a down payment on the tavern?''

"That took a while to register, didn't it? I have already moved the fan once because you didn't like it in the sunroom. Not again. You looked shocked. I wasn't exactly stripped when I sold the ranch. I knew enough to put some in reserve. I have money and I just sold a few investments, Jessica. And what I don't have, I'll earn. I like remodeling and building, feeling a structure take life in my hands, and I can do both. Danya doesn't want to manage the ranch and it's up for sale. My brother has said that he is looking at Amoteh, to be with family. Maybe he'll want to go into business with me, either at the tavern or in building. Now open the box."

"Why didn't you tell me you'd moved ahead with the deal, something you wanted so much?"

"Ellie's baby was coming. She was in false labor and then the real thing. You were in full swing, taking charge, bossing me around, shuttling your people in that new van, and at night you dropped into bed. I thought it could wait. You seemed so excited and happy, my little ramrod. And then you were tied up with business. Time just went by. It didn't seem important.''

"It was very important. Here I was thinking of ways to get to you, to make you see reason, when you— I wasn't too tired to—''

"Find me wherever I might be and make love? In the shower? On the floor in the kitchen?''

Jessica couldn't explain her overpowering need to make love with Alexi—rather, she could and had surprised herself. Her biological need to create a family was running almost fever high—thanks to Ellie and Mikhail's astounding love—the beauty of it had reached out to snare her. When Alexi had cradled newborn Sasha close to him, his expression tender, Jessica had known that he was meant to be a father.

Was it so bad to want everything? How could she possibly see herself fulfilled as a woman in love, who was loved, wanting what every other woman had wanted before her—

Except her mother. And Jessica deeply feared she would fail

the commitment of a mother to a child, just as her mother had failed....

"You just looked at me with that look—and you were there—and Alexi, I am not going to be distracted from the current topic."

"Then you admit—I can distract you. You love me and you want me. You need me."

"Yes, all yeses. I admit everything. I'm guilty." She shook her head and leaned back from the tug of Alexi's hand on her braid. "You have money," she repeated. "Here I have been worrying about you getting your dream, and you were—"

Alexi's head went back, his eyes narrowing. Jessica had become familiar with that expression of pride and disdain of a male who did not want financial help from a woman, let alone his lover. "I am capable of handling my finances. Do you think that I would ask the woman I love and want to marry to support me? Open it."

"Marriage? Love? Alexi, I—"

He sighed roughly and his words had the old-fashioned phrasing that said he was deeply touched. "I am emotional. Yes, I love you and I want to marry you. It just came out wrong. I'm sorry for that, but not that I want to marry you."

Shaken by his admission and uncertain that she could give Alexi what he deserved, Jessica looked away from those brilliant blue eyes that saw so much.

Alexi tipped her chin up and kissed her lightly. "Open the box," he whispered and lifted it to her.

Jessica placed the box on a table and opened it carefully, exposing a small patchwork quilt, beautifully embroidered with designs. She carefully lifted the edges aside and inside rested a large flat, obviously old, covered basket.

"My mother's," Alexi said, and eased the quilt and basket from the box. "She had just started this quilt when she passed. She asked me to give it to the woman I love. These are her needles and embroidery things."

His accent deepened, his hand running over the old basket slowly. "Once you said you learned to embroider from your grandmother and that she cared for you. You said you have nothing to remember her, but I thought perhaps you might like to have my mother's things.''

Alexi smiled softly, as if a fond memory had just touched his heart. From the folds of the quilt he lifted a child's well-worn red shirt, embroidered with flowers, and other children's clothing—soft and created with love. "Mine. She always embroidered my father's shirts—old-world fashion. But when Danya and I got older, we wouldn't wear them. She always wanted a girl.''

The enormity of the treasured gift overwhelmed Jessica. Her fingers slid over an oval embroidery hoop. "Alexi, I can't take these. They're too precious.''

But already Jessica was thinking of Ellie and Mikhail's new daughter, a perfect little blond, blue-eyed baby who had arrived just a month and a half ago. Jessica had given the baby a Moses cradle, a long wicker basket with handles and padded with commercial machine embroidering—one with these old-world designs on the pillow around the sides and the bottom would be just perfect for Sasha Stepanov. Alexi had given a set of blocks, inset with his carvings of the alphabet letter and an item that a child would recognize.

"They are yours now. Use them, if you want." He touched a large, obviously cherished wooden hoop. "From my grandmother. My mother said it eased women and they could solve their problems while working through these designs—''

Caught by the enormity of the gift, a family treasure given to her, Jessica turned suddenly to Alexi. The words just flowed from her heart and over her lips. She'd never given them to anyone, but Robert, her dear friend, and to Willow. Given to Alexi, the meaning was richer, sparkling with colorful, fascinating facets of the future, and she knew she could never give them to another man. "I love you.''

He seemed to struggle with his emotions, tenderness mixed with pleasure. Jessica feared she had gone too far, because she hadn't really given Alexi anything but words, how she felt in her heart. Then he smiled softly and stroked her cheek. "I know you love me, but the words given to me are the best gift. I know that you are afraid and that you have a promise to keep and that you fear too much. Be brave. That is what I am here for—to listen—and yet you keep yourself from me—what hurts you inside. It is tearing you apart, Jessica. Let me help.''

She shook her head and gripped the old soft quilt, as yet unfinished. Her own mother had given her nothing. How could she possibly fit into this loving family? "You don't understand. I don't deserve any of this."

From inside a lace-edged handkerchief, tucked amid the embroidery basket, Alexi took a small, obviously old black-velvet box. He opened it slowly and spoke quietly, "From my mother's mother and hers before her."

In his big workman's hands, the diamond-shaped onyx stones gleamed amid the intricate design of tiny marcasite and crystals surrounding them. Feminine and fragile, the pieces were connected by gleaming chains in a harlequin pattern. Glittering and shifting with Alexi's hands, the large V-shaped necklace seemed almost warm and alive.

Alexi opened the sturdy clasp. "Turn around."

"Oh, no. I can't wear that." Another woman had loved it, had loved Alexi, a woman who knew how to give comfort and love and—

He turned her slowly and leaned down to whisper in her ear, "You always make a fuss. This is a small thing. Mom would have wanted you to have it. I want you to keep it."

"Alexi, this is a family heirloom."

When the necklace rested against her skin, Alexi studied her. He traced the border of the V-shape upon her sweatshirt and then lifted it to slide it inside—against her skin. "It belongs on your skin, such soft, pale skin. Wear it sometimes, will you?"

She stared helplessly up at him, her emotions trembling inside her. "Alexi, this is too much."

His eyes were blue and warm and tender, filled with dreams Jessica badly wanted to step into, with a life she couldn't possibly have. Or could she?

"I have said I love you. It is not too much. You give me so much more," Alexi whispered, his lips against hers.

* * *

Alexi had asked her to marry him.

She'd told him she loved him.

The enormity of that commitment, the simplicity of it, stunned Jessica. Was a future as Alexi's wife possible?

When Alexi left to work at the tavern, Jessica was alone. She held her breath and inserted the embroidery needle into the quilt block's flower design that Louise Stepanov had started years ago. The night was quiet, the fire crackling in the free-standing modern woodstove that had replaced the cookstove.

Marriage to Alexi, and everything that it meant to be his wife. The needle slid into the fabric and then the thread, and Jessica pulled slightly, trying to remember her grandmother's lessons. The stitches came to life with surprising ease.

She looked at the new floor they had laid together, the large wooden planks gleaming beneath the varnish. At the Stepanov shop, the planks had been cut from beams that had been discarded in the remodeling. The Stepanov men had worked together, sanding and finishing until the boards for the main room were finished.

Meanwhile, Jessica had enjoyed sharing tea at Mary Jo's with Ellie and Leigh and Ed and Bliss. Tanya had played on the floor with her dolls and Katerina had slept in her mother's arms. It was a quiet time that Jessica had never had, sharing the things that made a woman's life.

Those times, visiting with Ellie in her new home and with Leigh, highlighted the emptiness of Jessica's own life.

She slid the needle into the fabric and, as she worked, watched the petals of the flower grow.

She had an obligation to Robert: *Take care of my son, will you, Jessica? I wasn't the father I should have been.*

Alexi deserved a full-time wife; Jessica knew he wouldn't tolerate Howard's threats or interference in their lives. Alexi wanted so little and yet deserved so much.

Jessica began embroidering a little bud, just one petal open, next to the completed flower. The bud seemed to symbolize a new life waiting for her to open it. *She loved Alexi.*

But there was so much inside her that she hadn't met, the

bitterness of her family, that very private part she kept from everyone, the part that had made her disbelieve in everything that she'd found true in Amoteh—that families loved each other and cared for their children, prizing them.

For the next hour Jessica gave herself to the intricate design, flowers and buds on a long waving vine. Focused on her stitches, she let all the strain of running a big corporation drain out of her. She loved Alexi. Was that enough? "Alexi…"

Jessica carefully placed aside her work and rose to study herself in the full-length oval mirror framed by wood; it was a new Stepanov design. She carefully protected the necklace as she eased away her clothing, letting it pool to the floor.

She shook her hair free of its ponytail, ran her fingers through it and studied her tousled look in the mirror. The large V-shaped necklace glittered at her throat, and two months of Alexi had changed that stark, tense look around her eyes and mouth.

Jessica traced her nude body. It was softer now, fuller in her breasts and hips, sensitized by just the thought of how Alexi touched her. His large, roughly callused workman's hands would run smoothly over her body, intimately sliding within… "Alexi," she whispered again.

Her emerald wedding band glittered on the hand resting over the necklace. A slow, sweet memory slid through her of a loving man who cherished her—her friend, her mentor, Robert. Ailing badly when they had married, Robert wanted her away from overt and painful gossip, and under the protection of his name. And then one dismal rainy day, she was alone, fighting Howard and running a corporation.

Circled by tender memories of Robert, Jessica slowly moved around the house, turning off the lamp. She gathered all the candles she could find and placed them around the living room. With the candles lighting the room, Jessica removed the ring and placed it in a small box. "Sleep well, Robert. You'll always be in my heart."

Jessica ran her hand over the secretary desk that Alexi had created just for her. Then she opened the drawer and slid the box within.

When she turned to the slight sound of a door opening, she found Alexi—big, vibrant, hair wind-tossed and silvery eyes stroking her body, heating it. "It is no small thing that you say you love me," he stated unevenly as he removed his coat. "It is no small thing that I ask you to be my wife. It is not a night to stay away from you. I thought I heard you calling my name and I came to you. I will always come to you. I will always love you."

Alexi didn't want to frighten Jessica. The feverish need to lock his body with hers, to physically merge with her, a woman he loved, was too strong. "I love you," she'd said earlier.

He knew that her words, given freely to a lover, were new to her lips. She'd probably said them as a teenager and as a friend to a dying man and to Willow. But to Alexi, they had been given as a woman's truth to a man who had her heart.

Alexi had heard Jessica's voice, that soft whisper calling him, over the sound of music and the tavern's customers. Seeing her now, with her hair waving softly around her face, her eyes dark and mysterious, and wearing only his mother's necklace, his heart raced. In the candlelight dancing upon Jessica's pale, curved body, her reddish hair, the feminine jewelry looked almost pagan.

"Alexi…" Her whisper was the same as he had heard beckoning him—soft, sensuous, longing.

With graceful movements, Jessica turned to blow out the candles placed everywhere around the room.

When one remained alight, she picked up the candlestick holder and turned toward the bedroom they had created together. Her hair shifted upon her back, that long, sweet, sensuous back, her hips swaying above legs that were slender and yet strong.

Alexi removed his clothes and slowly walked to her. Inside the large bedroom, the floor's gleaming wooden planks covered by temporary area rugs, a candle burned on top of the tall sturdy Stepanov dresser. In front of the mirror, Jessica stood, her hands busy with the necklace's clasp.

"Leave it on," Alexi ordered roughly, and when she turned

to him, a protest on her lips, he bent to lightly kiss her. His hand flattened over the necklace, over the woman he wanted to keep forever. "Please."

With a sigh, she lifted her slightly parted lips to his, and Alexi's hand slid lower to cup and caress her breast. The brush of his thumb across her nipple drew her sharp breath, her hands smoothing his tense shoulders. Then her fingers dug in to lock upon him and Alexi felt the immense rush of heat from her, the hunger burning him. With his arms around her, Alexi walked her slowly back to the bed, to the covers and sheet she had turned back.

"Say it," he demanded roughly, needing once more to hear those stunning words that told him of her love.

"I love you."

It was enough to send them tumbling into the bed, both hurrying for the physical completion. Then Alexi was sliding into her, her body welcoming his and the passion rising fever-hot between them.

"Alexi…" she whispered yearningly against his lips, beckoning to the equal hunger within him. "Alexi…"

Ten

From the cliff trail above the beach, Alexi braced his body against the late March winds. He watched the woman walking on the sand below; Jessica seemed small against the wide expanse of ocean, the overcast afternoon sky.

In low tide, the brown stretch of sand was rimmed by driftwood carried by the waves and deposited on the shore. Jessica made her way slowly around the dark clumps of seaweed, stopping occasionally to pick up a shell, studying it.

As she turned to study the ocean and the jutting black rock rising out of it, wind pushed her jacket against her, her hair confined beneath Alexi's knitted cap. With Deadman's Rock a distance from shore, the passage between it and land was dangerous in high tide. Deadman's Rock had cost many lives, including Jarek's first wife.

In low tide, Strawberry Hill could easily be reached by motorboat or walking higher on the shore. On that peninsula that jutted out into the Pacific Ocean, Kamakani had once looked down at a land he'd hated, cursing it as he died.

Alexi wondered if Kamakani's curse would eventually take Jessica away from him. He swallowed roughly; she might be preparing to leave him. Jessica was clearly troubled, silently at work with her needle in the evenings and awake and restless long into the night. He could hear her typing on her laptop, the muffled sounds of a tiny portable printer followed by a shredder chewing paper.

But her struggle seemed to lie inside, a sadness that came to her in the midst of a Stepanov family tea. It lay in her silence as she wrapped herself in the soft, woven throw and stood on the deck, surveying Amoteh and the Ocean; it lay in the way she held baby Sasha close and tender against her. Jessica's quiet distraction at times had nothing to do with business, rather with an ache and a struggle she would not share with Alexi.

She loved him. Alexi was certain of that fact. It was in the way she leaned against him, touched him, made long, lingering love to him—almost as if she were storing the memories of him.

If she loved him, how could she hold herself away from him? Waiting for her to trust him, to tell him what wrapped her so darkly within it, was more difficult than fighting anything physical—something he could battle in his two hands and make right for her.

Small and alone, she stared up at him as though she'd known he would be there....

Then she turned and walked back toward Amoteh, the ocean's waves framing that small figure hunched against the wind.

Was that how she would walk away from him? The tide erasing her footprints in the sand as if she'd never lain in his arms? As if he'd never found heaven in hers?

He could only wait and, for a Stepanov male, leashing his instincts to protect his love was the most difficult task of all.

"I made this before the baby came. I must have sewed miles then. It's nothing really, just an idea," Ellie said as the four women stood in her sewing room. After what was becoming a very special tea for the women, Leigh, Willow and Jessica watched as Ellie carefully removed a box from beneath folded layers of material. "I want this to be a surprise. We can make this happen, if you all are with me—and even Mikhail doesn't know. He gets all nervous when he comes in my sewing room. He looks like he's afraid the lace and thread will get him. He had a battle once with my serger and it got the best of him.... I can handle a sewing machine, but give me an embroidery hoop and a needle and I'm all thumbs. Between us, I thought we could do this...."

She spread out the man's large shirt on her worktable and studied it critically. She adjusted the flowing sleeves and the wide collar. "I've made Mikhail regular shirts before and Alexi is about his same size. Since only Jessica can embroider well now, she's elected to help the rest of us. It's the best I could do from the old-world pictures of the Stepanov ethnic festival shirts. Mary Jo enlarged the pictures and printed them so that you can see the original embroidery pattern better. Louise used to make these shirts. I thought maybe Jessica would teach us how to embroider like she does."

"I would love to learn how to do that," Leigh said. "I want Katerina to have a little something special on her clothes, from me to her."

She smoothed her rounded belly. "By the time this baby comes in August, I hope to do well enough to embroider a baby blanket."

Willow's eyes lit as she smoothed the fabric. "This shirt is gorgeous. I wish I could sew or do something like this. I didn't know Jessica could embroider so well until lately. I never thought of her as a...well, artistic craft-type person. I mean, she's painted my toenails, but she has a real eye for color. Who would know?"

She looked up and grinned at Jessica. "I mean, you always seemed so locked into your work. You've changed. Here you are, running the shuttle and working with Alexi—"

"I wasn't born a corporate fiend, you know, Willow. And

I'm still working. I have to make a statement before the board next week—''

"Lose that job," Willow stated fiercely. "It was eating you, and that nut Howard is—"

Jessica frowned at Willow, effectively stopping her next words.

Ellie took Jessica's hand. "I may not seem like it now, but I was in business with my father—a pretty ruthless guy. He's changed and so have I. Don't turn your back on what you can have with Alexi, Jessica."

"I made a promise that I can't forget. I can't throw it away."

"You'll do the right thing," Leigh said. "Love has a way of bringing priorities to the top."

"You need to think of yourself, Jessie," Willow said softly, and kissed Jessica's cheek. "Just for once. You're happy here and you know it."

Drawn to the shirt, Jessica's mind was working, traveling over the color and the stitches, to make the designs come to life. "Viktor sent Alexi's boyhood clothes. I can get some of the designs…. For Alexi?"

"Yes, and for you," Ellie said with a hug. "You've been spending a lot of time with that needle, and I only hope it is settling whatever is bothering you. Sewing did that for me when I was struggling with how I could manage as Mikhail's wife. We need someone like you to work on the first one—a pilot project, so to speak."

"I don't think I am right for Alexi," Jessica stated quietly. The enormity of being included in a family project, one created out of love, stunned her.

"I think you are. More importantly, he evidently thinks so, too. It's in the way he looks at you and how you look at him."

"I love him. But there are things—"

Ellie rocked Jessica in her arms. "Love is the important thing, isn't it?"

"Oh, gosh," Willow warned. "Jessie is going to cry. She's been doing a lot of that lately, and I'll bet Alexi doesn't know. I think she's been holding those tears for years."

"He's asked me to marry him. I can't, not until—"

"Old baggage," Willow explained solemnly to Leigh and Ellie. "She hasn't figured out how to handle it yet, but she will."

At the same time, Alexi was going over figures in the home office he and Jessica shared. Drawn by the constant electronic beeping alarm, Alexi worked free the jammed paper from Jessica's small printer. He noted that other faxed papers lay curled on the floor beneath the desk. The faxes generally arrived in the evening, while Jessica was working at her small desk.

Her laptop, through which the faxes had been transmitted, had sprung to life, and Alexi quickly noted a roster of past ones—all from Howard.

In straightening the paper from the floor, he noted Howard's furious handwritten note: *Don't play games with me, Jessica. You've been trying to make me choose between my wife and you for years. It cost me a fortune to get rid of her, but I did. You owe me. H.*

Alexi scowled as he read the rest of the faxes, all intimidating Jessica.

And from the inferences, she had been replying, refusing to meet Howard and warning him away from Amoteh.

Alexi had noted that stiffening of her body, that quick frown before she placed the faxes into her shredder. After the first fiery anger at a man who would try to intimidate a woman, Alexi sank into another thought—Jessica did not trust him to open the corners of her life.

When Jessica entered the house, flushed with the spring day, Alexi stood still, battling his emotions. She grinned at him as if she were a child bursting with a secret.

She had one, all right, Alexi thought darkly as she stood on tiptoe to kiss him. "Hi."

He met the kiss and then moved away. "Your printer was jammed. I cleared it. Your faxes are on the desk."

"I told them to send them at night, when I'm working—" Jessica frowned at Alexi. "What's wrong?"

He motioned to the desk and Jessica hurried to read the faxed notes from Howard. Her face pale now, she turned to Alexi. "Alexi, I never promised Howard anything."

She'd hurt him, and he lashed out at her in quick, cutting words. "You don't trust me."

Her eyes rounded and her voice was uneven as she said, "Alexi, I trust you with my life—"

The slice of his hand cut through the rest of her sentence. Deeply emotional, Alexi's accent framed his words. "You trust me so much that you don't tell me when another man has been threatening you."

"Howard hasn't threatened me."

"He's a centimeter from doing so. His expectations are high. And you didn't think enough of me, of what we have, to tell me that he was pushing you."

"Alexi, I want all that away from here. I've got a new life here—"

He inhaled sharply. "You think that I am here only in the good times. That I will protect you and love you only when you allow? You never come to me for comfort when you are troubled. Instead, you go inside yourself where no one can reach—where my love cannot reach you. How am I supposed to deal with that? You think this is how it should be between a man and a woman?"

Jessica shook her head and braced her body in a way that Alexi understood—she had set her mind. "Howard belongs to another world. I want to keep him there."

"So that is why you go back—to deal with him." A new thought stunned Alexi and he delivered it heavily wrapped in his accent. "You think...you think that you are protecting me, don't you?"

"You have a bit of a temper, Alexi—"

He stared coldly at her, a shield for his bleeding heart. "Do you know how hard it is for me not to go to Howard right now?"

"Yes, I do," she whispered. "Please don't."

"You are asking me to step back—from a man who considers you his property? Who could be dangerous to you?"

Incredibly, to Alexi's way of thinking, Jessica nodded. "I love you, Alexi. Please."

Please. It was the first time Jessica had said the word, had pleaded with him so desperately. The word went through his pride like a sword. With a curt nod, Alexi walked out of the house.

He didn't turn back as Jessica called his name— "Alexi..."

He was striding on the beach, battling his frustration, when something hit him lightly in the back. Alexi turned briefly to see Jessica standing a distance away from him, breathing as if she had been running. The child's ball she'd thrown was Tanya's, and discarded, it rolled on the sand. "Will you stop walking so fast?" Jessica asked between breaths.

Wrapped in a storm of love and pride and fear for her, Alexi folded his arms. He watched her walk toward him. "Your expectations of me are high, dearest."

Looking up at him now, Jessica said, "I know this isn't easy for you, Alexi. But I'm asking just that."

"Okay."

"You're almost breathing fire. That answer was too easy."

"Not for me. I want your promise that if Howard makes any kind of a move—one that might endanger you, that you'll tell me."

"I will. Alexi, please don't be angry. I—"

Alexi rubbed his jaw with his open hand. A woman's tears could disable him, and Jessica's, threatening to spill down her cheeks, were twice as potent. "If you can handle Howard, what else is bothering you?"

She shook her head and Alexi tilted her face up to his. "What else?"

"Don't you see? I could be like my mother—not a molecule of motherly instinct—"

He shook her head gently. "Is that what's troubling you?"

"You're a Stepanov. Look at Jarek and Mikhail. You're just like them. You should have a family...children. What if I—?"

"I think you are taking a lot on yourself. If we remodeled a house together, and survived that, I think we can surely work through whatever life brings us."

"You make it sound so simple. And you're a real complication—one that I love, but, Alexi, I want the best for you. I don't know that I am what you should have—"

"Do what you have to do. I love you." Alexi drew her closer and leaned his forehead on hers. "Okay?"

"Okay," she answered unevenly.

"Of course," he prompted in the typical Stepanov phrase.

"Of course."

With only a few days left before she had to return to Seattle for the board meeting, Jessica eased the shuttle van close to Mrs. Talbert's sidewalk and parked. She opened the handicap door and helped the woman in a wheelchair ease from the van. On the sidewalk now, Mrs. Talbert carefully opened her black purse and gave Jessica two dollars. Payment wasn't necessary, but Jessica realized that the elderly woman's pride was important. She pushed the wheelchair onto the house's ramp, and as Mrs. Talbert entered the house, Jessica retrieved the sacks of groceries.

Finished with her day's deliveries, and after a tea break with Willow, Jessica scanned the late-afternoon sun. She had just enough time to work in the herb bed she had started recently and, after dinner, Alexi was working at the tavern and she'd curl up to work on his shirt. *Alexi, the man she loved, who understood her need to work through her own life, though his instincts told him to take charge....*

The smile on her lips went deeper, warming her heart. She placed the van in gear, and when she arrived at the house, she saw Howard.

He stood beside his sports car, his hands on his hips, surveying the house that Alexi and she had remodeled. With the feeling that it was time to end Howard's relentless pursuit, Jessica braced herself for the battle.

She walked toward him just as Alexi came out of the house. He crossed his arms and leaned against a cedar post. But Jessica knew that easy stance hid Alexi's instincts to protect her, to let her finish one phase of her life her way.

Alexi nodded to her and the grim set of his expression told her that he wouldn't interfere—but he wasn't leaving her alone. Jessica nodded back at him and met Howard's furious stare. "Howard."

"You left my father's mansion for this?" he demanded. He glanced disdainfully at Alexi, who hadn't moved, and then back to Jessica. His gaze went down her loose sweatshirt, torn a bit from maneuvering wheelchairs, to the dirt on her jeans from gardening to the mud on her work boots. "You moved in with this down-on-his-luck bartender? What is he going to say when he finds out that you deserted a family who needs you? That you've been paying them off for years to keep away from you?"

"That's going to end, Howard. So is any contact with you. Alexi knows everything."

He sneered at that. "You can't cut off communications with me. I hold a good share of the company. And you're a gold digger. You won't walk away from everything my father built—or the money. You're just having a fling, but you'll come back and—"

"I'm walking away from everything, Howard. I am going to announce that at the board meeting. James Thomas and his son are stepping into my position. You'll have to deal with them—"

His openmouthed, stunned expression was comical. "You don't mean that."

"The attorneys are at work on it now. I'll sign the papers when I arrive. It's time you stood on your own, Howard. Your life now is what you make of it, just like I'm going to stay here in Amoteh—with Alexi. I'm going to marry him."

When Howard moved angrily toward her, Alexi straightened and moved down the steps. "Are you finished, Jessica?"

"Yes. Goodbye, Howard." With that, Jessica walked toward Alexi and his arm circled her waist as they watched Howard's sports car race out of sight.

Jessica leaned close to Alexi and placed her arms around his waist. She leaned her head against his shoulder, nestling into its strength and comfort. "Howard has always been able to see reality, especially when he stands to lose money. In his will, Robert provided that if I ever wanted to leave my duties as executrix, James Thomas would take my place. James and his son will manage Sterling Shops better than I ever could, and Howard knows it. James is going to continue minimal payments to my parents and see that they have health care. I still love them, Alexi, but love isn't being used by those who should love you.''

Alexi held her closer. "I'm going to that board meeting with you.''

"Okay," she said simply.

"You need me.''

"I know.''

Alexi eased her away slightly and frowned down at her warily. "That was too easy.''

"I thought I'd give you a break. You're an emotional kind of guy. I'll hold your hand through the tough parts and we'll celebrate later. I'll buy you chocolate and flowers.''

He snorted at that, an image no Stepanov male would like, the reverse of the male-female roles. Then a lovely reddish hue rose up his tanned cheeks. "You are teasing, of course.''

"Of course. But I do have a very special present for you.''

"Give it to me at our wedding.''

After the board meeting, Jessica studied the man driving the big, weathered pickup. The vehicle contrasted with Alexi's navy blue suit, light blue shirt—open now at the collar, with the pin-striped tie tucked into his pocket. In a whirlwind of three days, this new Alexi fitted into business schedules, efficiently clearing the way in the smaller details, so that Jessica could quickly end one phase of her life and begin another with him. He took her frustration and her orders with only a nod, carrying them out as if he'd always been a corporate man.

April's sunshine spread over the green pastures on the way to Amoteh, and then the Pacific Ocean appeared in a sliver of blue-gray meeting the same shade of sky. A sailboat's white sails skimmed that narrow edge between land and water, and Jessica settled into the feeling of home. She felt so light and young and happy, and Alexi was perfect to tease.

She stroked his cheek and smiled when he turned slightly to

kiss her fingertip. "You're gorgeous, Alexi Stepanov. A real dreamboat."

He frowned and that proud tilt of his head said he rejected the compliment. "A man is not gorgeous. This is Mikhail's suit. I'll wear it when we marry—soon. No more than a month."

"Oh, you're setting schedules for me, are you?"

"Yes. I know that you have to see for yourself what you have left, to remind yourself why you had to survive. A trip to your parents will only take a few days—"

"I want to go alone."

"No, that's out of the question."

He shouldn't have let Jessica return to her childhood alone; it would tear her apart. Alexi stood on Strawberry Hill, looking at the wide expanse of mid-April sky and water. In the distance, Amoteh was beginning to stir with tourists. His father had decided that the finished house was meant for Jessica and Alexi, and was temporarily living with Fadey and Mary Jo. Viktor fully enjoyed family life around him. The Stepanov house blared with loud music and the reunited brothers danced and hugged and laughed. The teas were quiet with memories shared, while children listened and played on their laps.

Alexi let the wind stir in his hair and thought of the woman he loved. In the night, he'd sense her calling his name—"Alexi…"

The wind seemed to carry her voice now and Alexi frowned—Jessica was really calling his name. "Alexi…"

He turned to see her walking toward him, her body pale and curved and nude beneath the long coat she had opened. His necklace glittered on her throat, V-ing lower onto her chest.

Alexi understood her solemn expression as she came nearer, her green eyes never leaving him as she began to dance in front of Kamakani's grave. She would tell him later of what she'd felt and what had passed, but she had finally ended her guilt, putting aside the past's ghosts; then Jessica walked toward him and their future together.

* * *

Alexi looked at the woman, dressed traditionally, walking toward him on the beach.

He smoothed the shirt she had embroidered for him, his hand flowing over the designs that might seem too ornate for a man. He looked at his cousins, Mikhail and Jarek, all dressed in the same design, with a large collar, sleeves that billowed in the fresh, salty, ocean air. The embroidered designs seemed alive and warm, and each had been carefully planned and given by a woman in love. Alexi prayed that his brother, Danya, standing at his side would find a love who would embroider his plain shirt.

Tears shimmered in his father's eyes and in his uncle's— and perhaps, in his own, of course.

Unable to wait for Jessica to cross the distance to him, Alexi walked toward her. She welcomed him with a kiss and a blush that curled around his heart.

Jessica leaned close to him for just that moment that told him she needed him.

And then they walked toward the future.

"Take it off," Jessica demanded as Alexi carried her into their home.

"But I love it. I'm never taking off this shirt," he teased as he dropped her on their bed amid a flurry of lace and satin and flowers and love.

She tugged him down and placed the bridal headpiece, a circlet of flowers, over his head, then raised to straddle him. "I love you, Alexi Stepanov."

He grinned and began to unbutton the shirt she had embroidered for him. "Of course."

DYNASTIES: THE DANFORTHS

A family of prominence...
tested by scandal, sustained by passion.

COWBOY
CRESCENDO
(Silhouette Desire #1591)

by **Cathleen Galitz**

Newly hired nanny Heather Burroughs quickly
won over Toby Danforth's young son with her
warmth and humor, but Toby's affection was
harder to tap into. This sizzling cowboy was
still reeling from his disastrous divorce and
certainly wasn't looking for a new bride.
Could Heather lasso this lone rancher
and get him to settle down?

Available July 2004
at your favorite retail outlet.

Enjoy
Barbara McCauley's

SECRETS!

**Hidden passions are revealed
in this next exciting installment
of the bestselling series.**

MISS PRUITT'S PRIVATE LIFE
(Silhouette Desire #1593)

Brother to the groom, Evan Carter was
immediately attracted to a friend of the bride:
sexy TV sensation Marcy Pruitt. While helping
to pull the wedding together, they found
themselves falling into a scandalous affair.
But when Miss Pruitt's private life became
public knowledge, would their shared passion
result in a wedding of their own?

*Available July 2004
at your favorite retail outlet.*

Silhouette® Desire®

BABY AT *HIS* CONVENIENCE

by
Kathie DeNosky

(Silhouette Desire #1595)

Katie Andrews wants a strong, sexy
man to father her child. When former
marine sergeant major Jeremiah Gunn
walks into her café, Katie believes she's
found the perfect candidate. Trouble is,
Jeremiah has some conditions of his
own before he'll agree to give Katie
what she wants—including turning sweet,
shy Katie into the type of brazenly
uninhibited woman he's used to.

*Available July 2004
at your favorite retail outlet.*

COMING NEXT MONTH

#1591 COWBOY CRESCENDO—Cathleen Galitz
Dynasties: The Danforths
Newly hired nanny Heather Burroughs quickly won over Toby Danforth's
young son with her warmth and humor, but Toby's affection was harder to
tap into. This sexy cowboy was still reeling from his disastrous divorce and
wasn't looking to involve himself in any type of relationship. Could Heather
lasso this lone rancher into settling down?

#1592 BEST-KEPT LIES—Lisa Jackson
The McCaffertys
Green-eyed P.I. Kurt Striker was hired to protect Randi McCafferty and
her baby against a mysterious attacker. After being run off the road by this
veiled villain, Randi had the strength to survive any curve life threw her.
But did she have the power to steer clear of her irresistibly rugged
protector?

#1593 MISS PRUITT'S PRIVATE LIFE—Barbara McCauley
Secrets!
Brother to the groom Evan Carter was immediately attracted to friend of the
bride and well-known television personality Marcy Pruitt. While helping to
pull the wedding together, they found themselves falling into a scandalous
affair. But when Miss Pruitt's private life became public knowledge, would
their shared passion result in a wedding of their own?

#1594 STANDING OUTSIDE THE FIRE—Sara Orwig
Stallion Pass: Texas Knights
Former Special Forces colonel and sexy charmer Boone Devlin clashed
with Erin Frye over the ranch she managed and he had recently inherited.
The head-to-head confrontation soon turned into head-over-heels passion.
This playboy made it clear that nothing could tame him—but could an
unexpected pregnancy change that?

#1595 BABY AT *HIS* CONVENIENCE—Kathie DeNosky
She wanted a strong, sexy man to father her child—and waitress
Katie Andrews had decided that Jeremiah Gunn fit the bill exactly.
Trouble was, Jeremiah had some terms of his own before he'd agree
to give Katie what she wanted…and that meant becoming his mistress….

#1596 BEYOND CONTROL—Bronwyn Jameson
Free-spirited Kree O'Sullivan had never met a sexier man than financier
Sebastian Sinclair. Even his all-business, take-charge attitude intrigued
her. Just once she wanted Seb to go wild—for her. But when the sizzling
attraction between them began to loosen *her* restraints, she knew passion
would soon spiral out of control…for both of them.

SDCNM0604